CAPTIVE

A GRACED STORY

OTHER BOOKS BY AMANDA

THE GRACED SERIES

CAPTIVE

A GRACED STORY

AMANDA PILLAR

MAATKARE
BOOKS

Published by Maarkare Books
www.amandapillar.com

Editor: Julia Knapman

ISBN: 978-0-6480295-2-6

Cover Design: Ljiljana Romanovic © 2016
Internal Layout: Amanda Pillar © 2016

First Published February 2016

To Tom

PROLOGUE

A long time before the events in Graced...

The world's in ruins around me. I was born in a time of war, and knew civilization was always doomed to go in one direction, and it certainly wasn't up. It makes it hard to feel optimistic for your future, right? I've seen once proud cities crumble to dust, pulverized by bombs, and then cannibalized for their precious materials, so that another town may endure. How long can humanity and their cousins, the Graced, survive the weres and the vampires?

So few cities – towns, really – are left, running on bootlegged systems, with their all-important medical supplies stored and guarded like precious jewels. There aren't enough scientists left to make things like antibiotics anymore, let alone cure cancer or heart disease (laughably once humanity's biggest fear). And that's assuming there are any doctors around to do the curing. Medical professionals were either killed outright or kidnapped and held hostage early on in the war. I only know of a handful who are 'free,' and they've been trained in specialist labs, focusing on doing the one thing they can to preserve humanity: removing the immortal threat.

Destroying humanity's greatest creation.

But what about the rest of us?

I'm not human, nor am I immortal, so I really got the shit end of that deal. Humans had wanted the one thing they couldn't have: more time. Geneticists had experimented, splicing DNA, manipulating genes, cutting and snipping and culling until they ended up with a byproduct they hadn't predicted: my people, the Graced. The colors of our eyes eventually became synonymous with our abilities: Blue for empaths, Green for telepathy and Gray for telekinesis. Some were so strong, they could trigger devastating earthquakes, or make people into puppets, or even control mobs by turning their anger into bliss. I should know; I'm a Gray who could level a city if I wanted to.

And sometimes, I really want to.

My ability makes me feared, even by other Graceds. It's why I've never told my sisters how strong I am. They're only half-Graced – one with no ability due to her Hazel eyes, and one with a psychic touch so delicate, it can't even be used in self-defense. I don't want to see fear in their eyes when they look at me.

Even though my people were technically a failed experiment, scientists realized we may be the first step in achieving their ultimate goal. And so the trials continued, until one day, the first vampires and weres were born. Their weaknesses – the wood and silver allergies – had been coded into their genetics as a type of scientific joke, one that I think most people don't find particularly funny anymore. Especially since the only thing that sustains them is flesh and blood.

Human flesh and blood.

And that brings me back to the vampire-were war and the reason for it. It used to be a human/immortal war, but that changed a decade ago, after a plague decimated human and Graced populations. Now, the reason is simple: whoever controls the food source controls the world.

But Graceds are useful for more than one reason: we can breed with vampires and weres, increasing their numbers while reducing ours. So the immortals have extra motivation to capture one of us. Eventually though, humans may go extinct, and if that happens, the weres and vampires will also die out. It might actually be a blessing.

For now though, the creators are the hunted. A once proud race has been reduced to nothing more than cattle. Part of me doesn't care that humanity has been so cheapened; they're just reaping what they'd sown, after all. But my sisters are half-human, and that's not their fault. So I'll fight for them, at least while I can.

Nothing is more important than family, not even freedom.

~ Quin Kirkman, Journal

CHAPTER ONE

Dying is for the weak. Only the strong survive.
~ Quin Kirkman, Journal

"If you so much as blink, I'll rip your throat out."

The voice was deep and melodious and it took a moment for the words to register. But the cold steel of the blade pressed to her esophagus spoke louder. Laney held still. She doubted she'd ever been quite so motionless in her life. She was even holding her breath.

Laney's attacker was pressed to her back. He had one hand wrapped around her shoulders, the other holding the offending knife. She could feel his cold exhalations on her cheek, smell the stale blood on his breath.

Her eyes darted from side to side, trying to count how many vampires there were. All the humans had been herded into the village center, a patch of bare earth situated in the middle of their small settlement. Faces that were all the colors of humanity looked around at each other, some wild-eyed with fear, others resigned and worn. All of the eyes were Brown or shades thereof, except for the vampires, who had purple irises. She sought out her sister, hoping that she wasn't among those in the middle of the village.

A ring of wattle and daub huts lined the open area, spanning back three rows. Their settlement was on were lands; they should have been safe, at least from leech attacks. From the weres, not so much. She hoped Jane had managed to escape. On her second sweep, though, she met the worried Hazel gaze of her sister. A sinking feeling uncurled in her gut. Fear for herself, that was normal, but now she also had to worry about Jane.

"Take them all." That smooth tone again.

She counted four vampires in her field of vision, but there were probably more. They were dressed in military fatigues and had short haircuts – which would take constant maintenance, considering how fast their hair grew – and each carried an assault rifle and a large knife, not that they really needed them. Vampires were so fast they could knock out most humans before they had time to blink. Arms were unnecessary against a settlement of regular humans, which, as far as anyone was aware, was the case.

The weapons probably meant the vampires either thought there'd be weres here to protect the settlement, or they meant serious business. Laney feared it was the latter. If the weres had thought there'd be an attack, then the villagers would have been moved somewhere safe. And then there would have been a slaughter. The weres took their ownership over humans – their 'cattle' – *very* seriously.

Only Laney and one other villager were held physically captive by the vampires. Fear kept the others stationary. Her friends and sister stared at her with worried gazes. They wore a variety of drab dresses, pants and shirts. No one was outfitted for the cold weather, and she couldn't stop the involuntary shiver from traveling up her spine. The knife pressed closer to her throat. Looking up, she took in the sky overhead, gray and ominous; she bet it would rain within the next hour. Hopefully they were no longer out in the open when it happened.

The vampire's arm tightened around her shoulders before he let go and shoved her forward. She lost her balance and stumbled, only to be caught by some of the other villagers. Laney spun around and tried to take stock of the situation. It was worse than she'd thought. There were ten vampires and two large bio-fueled trucks. She could probably debilitate two or three, maybe four of the leeches. Maybe ruin one of the trucks. But she couldn't take on all of the vampires or destroy both trucks. She wasn't strong enough to do much more, half-breed that she was. Laney was just thankful that she still wore her contact lens. At least they had a secret advantage, if the time ever came for her to act.

The vampire who'd held her stared over the huddled villagers. His eyes were an icy, bright purple, his face a deep brown in contrast. His head was shaven, and he radiated a cold that was bone deep. She'd bet that he was second generation. That kind of emotionless state was bred into the early vampires. Not that there were all that many left after the wars. And the majority of those who were alive were third or fourth generation, at the earliest.

In the corner of her vision, near the ring of trees that surrounded the settlement, she spotted a figure lurking. She was surprised they hadn't been caught by the vampires; maybe the overwhelming smell of the settlement kept the spy hidden from their acute senses. She wondered if it was her brother, Quin, although he would have probably rushed in and tried to save them. It wasn't the first time that she wished she had one Green eye rather than one Gray. It's why she wore the contact lens, so they both appeared Brown. Her one colored eye meant she had some ability with telekinesis, but not enough to compete with a full-blooded Gray if there'd been one nearby. Yet, if she'd had one Green eye, she might have been able to communicate with the watcher. At least send a telepathic message. For now, she could only hope they would report back to the weres. Maybe they'd decide to come save them.

Then again, maybe they wouldn't.

"You are all property of the Raven Clan now. If you try to escape, you will be drained dry and left for the predators that lurk in the forests around your village. If you fight, you will be punished." The vampire grinned. "Trust me, you won't like the punishment, but we will."

CHAPTER TWO

I put my sisters in the safest place I could think of: a were compound. Sounds crazy, I know, but keeping them hidden in plain sight may just save them.
Some might say I should just stash them with Graceds, but too many of them hate humans beyond reason, even those who are only half-bloods.
~ Quin Kirkman, Journal

"They're all gone."

"What do you mean *gone*?" Wolfgang – or Wolf – demanded.

They were in the war room of a bunker that Wolf and his men had 'appropriated.' The room was about a hundred yards underground, with air shafts stretching upward into the black depths above. The vents on the surface were hidden with elaborate plantings, shields and all kinds of goodies that were irreplaceable now. The factories that had once built the technology were crumbling ruins, the scientists and engineers either dead or captured. There were very few 'free' humans left.

Actually, there were few humans at all.

Inside the compound, all the furniture was sleek glass and stainless steel, very vampiric, which is why Wolf enjoyed it so much. Anything he could steal from a filthy leech was better than anything he could buy from one. And he'd made sure that the vampire wouldn't be coming back to claim what was his. There was something altogether satisfying in ripping out a leech's throat. Even if their blood tasted like candy rather than dinner.

But unlike the wolf he was named for – and who he shifted into – Wolf didn't just kill to eat. He killed to survive, and sometimes, when a leech was involved, he killed for fun. Because there was only one race more fucked up than his: the vampires. He'd never met one that wasn't a born sociopath.

Wolf stood at one end of the conference room, a glass table stretching out before him, with a human and two guards positioned down the other end. The guards were dressed like him, in black clothing that had more sewn rips and tears than intact material. Clothing didn't survive a were's shapeshift, and with the constant fighting for land – and food – garb was the least of anyone's concerns.

Wolf strode forward, his steps purposeful. He met the tired Gray gaze of the man before him. Quin was Graced, and they were so rare now as to be almost mythical. They didn't normally side with vampires *or* weres; they were considered food, and often forced into being bedmates, since Graceds were the only race weres or vampires could breed with outside of their own.

"Gone as in taken." Quin was an ally of sorts. He helped them out from time to time, and they gave him a safe haven when he needed it. The man had never said why he offered his aid, and Wolf wasn't about to look a gift horse in the mouth. Perspiration dripped down from the Graced's forehead, pooling in a dusty puddle at his throat. The man stank of sweat and fatigue, but he stood on his own two feet. His telekinesis was probably keeping him upright. But you couldn't show weakness to a room full of predators, and Wolf respected the Graced for that. Not that Wolf trusted him, but there were few men, Graced, human or were, who he *would* trust. That's what happened when you were in the middle of a war. Especially a war that had been going on for almost as long as he'd been alive. Although the motivations had changed.

It took a few moments for Wolf to process what he'd been told. "*Who* took them?"

Quin snorted. "They didn't leave a calling card. But it's pretty easy to figure out."

Wolf growled into the stale, recycled air. "That fucking bastard!"

Wolf's territory was surrounded by two

other were groups, and one vampire clan. There was a peace treaty of sorts with the other weres: Wolf didn't touch their cattle if they left his alone. But the vampires didn't care about rules. Their appetites were growing uncontrollably. There was even talk of a merger – where all the vampire clans would band together to create some kind of super-clan to wipe out the weres once and for all. No competition for the cattle, then.

A new, deeper voice entered the conversation. "Marcus doesn't run the Blood Clan there anymore."

Trace, a werebear who shifted into the biggest black bear Wolf had ever seen, was standing at the entrance to the room, behind the two guards. His skin was so dark, light was simply absorbed; only the white of his eyes and teeth gave away his position in the dim corridor. And his smell. But a Graced would never notice that. The guards moved to the side to let the bear enter.

"They had a coup?" Wolf frowned. "Why didn't I know about this? We could have taken advantage of it."

Trace shook his head. "He was there one day, dead and gone the next."

"Great." Wolf shoved a hand over his dreadlocks. A new leech to deal with. He'd have to learn all their tricks and how to counter them. And somehow, he had to figure out how to get his cattle – humans – back. The clan had a number of separate settlements, but even the loss of one human meant someone would go hungry that month.

"Word is that Tatiana is now in charge of the newly named Raven Clan. She's also apparently taken control of the nearest three vamp clans."

Wolf froze, his hand tangled in his blond-brown hair.

Tatiana.

There were few vampire reputations that could really rattle Wolf, but hers was one of them. First generation, and insane as a cut snake. She could be charming and vivacious one minute, then ripping your still-beating heart out of your chest the next. All with a beautiful smile, framed by lush red lips.

"This is not good," Wolf said softly, lowering his hand, clenching it into a fist at his side.

"No shit," Quin quipped.

Everyone knew who Tatiana was.

"I thought she was dead," one of the guards said.

Trace shook his head. "Her son, Vincent, was staked in the last were attack on her previous fortress. She must have survived."

First generation weres and vampires were extremely hard to kill. And now that the last of her children had been eliminated...

"She's going to be out for revenge," Wolf said.

"The were who killed him is long dead," Trace commented.

Wolf shook his head. "Revenge for one such as her isn't limited to the killer. She'll be after every were who ever breathed in his direction." And his people were right in her line of fire.

"What about the humans?" Quin asked in the following silence.

"What about them?" Trace queried.

The Graced's Gray eyes almost glowed. The table began to shake. "We can't just leave them there! They'll become addicts. Shells of their former selves. Used for more than just food."

Wolf looked at him, really looked at the other man. Typically, Graceds didn't have a lot of time for humans, either. Humans were afraid of the other race; their thoughts, emotions and physical bodies were not theirs to control with a Graced nearby. So Graceds usually kept to themselves. Not wanted by anyone, except for breeding purposes.

"Why do you care?" Wolf asked.

Quin took a deep breath, exhaling slowly. "My sisters were in that settlement."

Both Trace and Wolf winced. "We can't just break into a vampire stronghold to get them out." Wolf blinked. "Wait – we had Graceds in one of my settlements? Why didn't you tell me?"

Quin bit his lip. "They're only half-Graced."

Trace folded his arms across his massive chest. "If you'd declared their race, they would have been removed and kept here, you know that. All potential breeding stock–"

"And that is why they were at the settlement." Quin's expression was shuttered. "My sisters were not there to be your personal broodmares. I thought they'd be safer here than with another were compound, or even with a Graced refuge. But they weren't."

Wolf frowned at the insult, but ignored it. If he had a sister, and they'd been abducted by a group of leeches, he'd be pissed as well. "If we get your sisters back, then you work with us from now on. Permanently." Having a Gray up their sleeve would be an invaluable asset.

"That's blackmail." Quin glared.

Wolf chuckled. "It sure is. Do we have a deal?"

CHAPTER THREE

Some days, I wish there was still proper alcohol. I could really do with a single malt whisky (or three), not this crap they call 'moonshine.'
~ *Quin Kirkman, Journal*

Laney's left eye ached. She'd been wearing her contact lens for over a month straight, which would have made her doctor throw a hissy fit, if he'd still been alive (she *could* wear them for days on end, but was meant to take them out and give them a clean). But he, along with her mother and stepfather and the rest of the city she'd grown up in – 'city' being a rather euphemistic description for the cobbled-together houses, bootlegged technology and ramshackle, half-demolished buildings that had been her home – were now nothing more than dust. Jane and Laney had only made it out before the attack on their home because of their half-brother, Quin. He'd come before the vampires and weres arrived and smuggled them out. How he'd known about the impending attack...Laney preferred not to speculate.

Usually, Graceds left their non-Graced siblings to rot, especially when they hadn't grown up together. But Quin had always watched out for them, if from a distance, and Laney could only hope he was doing the same now. He was a powerful Gray; he might stand a chance of breaking them out with his telekinesis.

Then again, he *had* dumped them in a were-controlled settlement where once every six months they were 'harvested' from. Every time they risked death at the hands of a were surgeon, whose only skill lay in removing the desired meat. Maybe Quin had thought that was the safest option. Why they couldn't stay with him, she'd never know. But then, she didn't really know much about how a full-blooded Graced thought, having never met any others, apart from her brother.

"My neck hurts," Jane said quietly.

Blinking, Laney realized her sister had returned from the selection. The vampire guard who had held the knife to Laney's throat had come into the dormitory and taken away six of the women. Laney imagined the same thing had taken place in the men's hall. It wasn't the first time this little trip had been orchestrated.

Instead of worrying about her sister, *like she should be,* she'd been off in her own little world. Which was dangerous – and stupid – in a place like this.

And Laney should be extra careful on behalf of her sister. Jane had Blue in her Hazel eyes. Being in a place like this, where cold-as-ice vampires roamed, feeding off humans who stank of fear…It'd be hard on someone like Jane, even though her gifts were latent. Sometimes Blue-Hazels had the ability to subconsciously pick up on the emotions of those around them. Luckily for Jane, it's probably why the vampires had left her with the 'herd'; Blues – empaths – weren't as desired as Greens and Grays for breeding stock.

Leaning down, Laney looked at her sister, who was sitting on the bottom bed of their metal bunk. Their bunk was tucked in the corner of the large steel and concrete warehouse; she had been given a false sense of security by the wall at her back. The sheets Jane and Laney sat on were a worn gray, with a threadbare woolen blanket neatly tucked over the top. Hopping down, Laney landed quietly on the concrete floor before sitting on the mattress next to her sister.

Jane had a hand clutched to her throat, where Laney could see a makeshift bandage protruding. It was dark red in the center, with pink tinges at the corners. Gently pulling aside Jane's hand, Laney looked at the wound. Trying to hide her wince, Laney met the tired Hazel eyes of her sister. Her straight, normally neat blonde hair had frayed from its bun.

"You need to get it cleaned."

There was no real reason why the wound should still be bleeding. Proteins in vampire saliva were designed to speed the human healing process from weeks down to a matter of hours. The vampire must have wiped the wound clean, to prevent healing. Or, whoever had fed didn't drool much while doing so.

Jane's gaze met hers. "I only have this rag."

Jane was the smartest person Laney had ever met. Not that there'd been a lot of people to meet when she'd been growing up, not by historical standards. A couple of thousand humans had called her shanty town home, before it became ruins. But it was enough for Laney to know Jane was far too intelligent for her own good.

"I'll go ask for help," Laney said.

Jane reached out and clasped Laney's wrist with her free hand. "No!" Then quietly, "It's okay. You know how to stop the bleeding. We don't want to draw attention to ourselves."

Laney looked down at the lightly tanned hand clutching her olive one. "It's not okay. If you get an infection, then there won't be antibiotics here to help."

At least, Laney seriously doubted there would be any kind of useful medication. Vampires didn't get infections. Plus, the production of medicines like that had been all but obliterated in the last ten years. Not enough humans to make them. Not enough facilities left standing. Things had gone past the point of no return a decade ago, after the plague had hit. Weres and vampires meant business now that the number of humans was dwindling down to thousands, rather than millions.

Humans were more valuable than gold.

Graceds even more so, since vampires and weres could breed successfully with them.

Standing, Laney shook off her sister's hand and walked to the door at the far end of the room. Her footsteps seemed to echo loudly in the concrete chamber, but since none of the other women appeared to pay her much attention, Laney figured she was being fanciful. Five of the other women clutched their necks with a dreamy expression on their faces, while the others sat wrapped in blankets. One or two spoke, but it was strangely silent in comparison to how life had been in the settlement.

Things hadn't exactly been fun while they'd lived under were control, but they'd had their own little wattle and daub house, complete with minimalistic wooden furniture one of the women had helped make, and meaningful if boring work. Laney and Jane had been in charge of running the vegetable gardens with some of the other women, while the men maintained the large crop fields, half of which were used to make the bio-fuel that ran the generators and vehicles. Although, the only use Laney had had for the generators was their ability to provide light and heat. Everything else had been done the old-fashioned way. But that single lightbulb that was lit for an hour each evening had allowed Jane and Laney to continue their real work, even if only theoretically.

Since they'd arrived at the Raven Clan, around a quarter of the female villagers had been used for food. Laney knew it was only a matter of time before she was taken out for a blood-letting session as well. As half-Graced, it was doubtful that she would be able to experience the high that the saliva could bring; she'd have to pretend through the pain. Learn how to mimic those glazed looks of happiness. Otherwise, their captors would soon work out what she was, and Laney didn't want to be a broodmare for some sociopathic vampire. She only hoped Jane had been a good actor; her sister would also become more than just food if they thought her Hazel genes were strong enough to resist the saliva high. Even if Blues weren't really wanted for breeding stock.

Reaching the huge metal door, Laney banged against the portal. It had a thick glass window, with the surrounding metal panels riveted together; she doubted her pounding would create too much of a ruckus, although it would give her a bruised fist. She stood patiently, waiting for someone to answer. While her efforts hadn't been that cacophonous, the vampires would still be able to hear her, even through the thick steel slab.

The door jerked open. "What?" The vampire on the other side of the door barked the question at her, his purple eyes ablaze. Laney hadn't seen him before, but that didn't mean much.

Fighting back the urge to cower, she looked in the general direction of the vampire's face. *Show no weakness,* she told herself.

"My sister needs medical treatment," Laney said, the words surprisingly confident.

The vampire bared his teeth, showcasing his long, curving fangs. Which were meant to be retractable. "Your sister can fuck off."

The vampire went to slam the door shut, but Laney shoved herself in the way. It was lucky he hadn't let go of the heavy metal slab, or she might have been crushed. "If you want her to get an infection, then go right ahead. Walk away. But I doubt you have the medical equipment to be able to stop the infection if it went to her blood, and then you've lost another piece of *cattle*." She spat the last word, and it made the vampire narrow his eyes. In thought, or annoyance, she couldn't tell. It was probably a bit of both.

The vampire looked her up and down.

"What would you know?"

"I'm a doctor." Sort of. Had been, over ten years ago. She'd graduated young, and had gone straight into clinical research. It was meant to have been a lifesaving goal. Something that would stop the war.

She'd been naive and stupid.

"What is wrong with her?" the guard asked.

"Whoever fed off her didn't leave enough saliva on the wound to make it heal. I either need you to spit on the bite – after I clean it – or get me some bandages so I can patch it up."

"So it is still bleeding?" The vampire pushed past her and strode into the large room. He slammed the door shut behind him. It was so heavy it would need two to three humans to move it. Purple eyes bored into her neck.

"Yes."

He snarled. "Idiots." Turning to her, the vampire demanded, "Where is she?"

Not the exact response she was after. Crossing her arms, she tried to radiate authority. As much as she could, as a captive, in the equivalent of a hessian sack and viewed as little more than dinner. "I need to clean it first, before you do anything to it."

She swore the vampire almost sighed. "What do you need to clean it?"

"Fresh bandages and saline."

"And this will prevent an infection?"

"It should." Hopefully. If they had any.

"Wait here. Make sure she doesn't lose too much blood, or you'll be fed from next."

CHAPTER FOUR

I have 'friends' everywhere. It keeps me alive.
~ Quin Kirkman, Journal

"We need to get them out." Quin folded his arms across his chest as he spoke. Trace, Wolf and the Graced were all seated in Wolf's office. It was a small room without a view, and had a desk, some filing cabinets and three chairs. All metal. One seat had been brought in from another room. Normally, Wolf used the office to chat to Trace alone; it was the only place he could be assured that the other weres wouldn't interrupt them, or hear what was said. There was only one 'soundproof' – when it came to were hearing – room in the whole underground compound, and this was it.

"What, you want us to just walk into the vampire fortress and ask for your sisters nicely?" Wolf didn't stop the sarcasm from lacing his words. He wanted the humans back as well, but some things you had to write off as a lost cause.

After all, they had another dozen settlements they could still harvest from, even if it meant this month a were or three may go hungry at the loss. They were making sure that the women who were fertile focused on becoming pregnant: gravid women were rewarded with more food, no harvesting, and private quarters with small luxuries. Plus, there was the whole benefit of the continuation of the human species. Although, the humans didn't seem to be too keen on producing young that would grow up to be food.

Part of him couldn't blame them.

But while Wolf had agreed to get the two girls out earlier, he was regretting it now. There was really no good plan. Offering the vampires two other replacement humans would do no good; the vampires would just want to know why *these two* were so important. And then they'd demand a settlement or three in return. And probably send back corpses.

"There's got to be something we can offer them," Quin muttered.

"Tatiana doesn't do deals," Trace said.

Trace would know. He was the public eyes and ears of their clan. While people knew that Wolfgang Fenris was the 'alpha,' he never ventured out in public under his real name. If you didn't know the face of the man you had to kill, then assassination was more difficult. And it was easier for him to hide his identity in comparison to some other weres, with him being second generation, rather than first – like most alphas or clan leaders. His details had never been stored in a lab report somewhere.

"We need to get someone inside then," Wolf mused, running a hand over his bristle-covered chin.

"They'd never make it out alive," Trace countered.

Quin sat up straight. "I'll go."

"Didn't know you had a death wish, or wanted to be a father so bad," Wolf said.

If a Gray Graced went into a vampire compound, they'd either become food or breeding stock. Probably both. They'd never get out alive.

"They wouldn't be able to contain me." Quin's voice had a cold seriousness that Wolf believed. But there were ways even Graceds could be stopped.

"Really?" Wolf stood. He motioned for Quin and Trace to follow him as he headed out the door. They entered a cool and sterile corridor that was typical of the compound: concrete walls, floors and ceilings with metal supports and doors. Wolf led them down a few more floors to a sub-level of the underground compound. This area had only a single corridor, lined with doors. Behind each door was a cell. The first six were designed to hold humans, the second ten for vampires or weres, and the last four were for Graceds. Supposedly. He hadn't had a chance to test the theory out.

Wolf turned back. "Follow me."

Reaching the last door, he opened it and motioned Quin to go inside.

The Graced stared at him. "Are you freaking kidding me?"

"This is an ex-vampire stronghold. This room is meant to be able to contain Graceds of all abilities. Try it out. I need to shut the door for the test to work properly. I won't lock it."

Quin just stood there. "You're asking me to trust you right now."

Wolf met the serious Gray gaze. "I guess I am."

It was a lot to ask someone, someone who could be held prisoner here and then used for whatever purposes Wolf wanted. But he needed an active Gray more than he needed an imprisoned one.

"In or out?"

They stood in silence for a handful of heartbeats, then Quin walked into the cell. "Close it."

Wolf shut the door, carefully making sure that he hadn't locked it.

Through the glass window, Wolf watched as Quin stood alone in the empty room, a look of concentration on his face, his eyes narrowed. But nothing seemed to be happening. His expression turned into a frown, and then Quin was gesticulating with his hands. Eventually he stopped. He walked to the door and tugged it open.

"I couldn't do *anything*." Surprise was evident on the man's face.

Trace looked contemplative. "I always wondered if these cells would work."

"I didn't know they had this kind of technology." Quin looked worried.

"I think only a few bases have it. But you can bet that Tatiana will have access to at least one of these. If you got trapped inside one, you couldn't get out unless someone let you."

"How does it work?"

"Buggered if I know," Wolf replied. He wasn't a scientist. But he could read the schematic diagrams he'd found and that's how he knew this was here.

Quin ran a hand over his face. "Fuck."

"Suddenly realizing how this is a game changer?" Wolf asked.

"It explains why some people have been taken and no one's heard of them again. We just assumed they were dead. Now, we may learn that they're not. Was anyone here when you took over the facility?"

"No one alive and no Graceds."

The former prisoners had all been found dead in the cells. Three weres had been locked in contorted positions, skin blue; Wolf had guessed some kind of silver-laced gas. The humans had been stiff as boards, their faces bleak. There'd been no Graceds. Maybe they had been taken out before the slaughter, because they were worth too much.

"All the more reason for me to go in," Quin said into the quiet.

"Are you *insane*?" Trace blurted.

"There could be more of my people in Tatiana's stronghold."

"There is no way we are going to risk you on something like this."

"I can't trust anyone else."

"I'll go," Wolf found himself saying.

Trace growled. "Have you lost your mind?"

"No one knows my face."

"I'm surrounded by idiots." Trace gnashed his teeth. "You're the *alpha*."

"I'm *one* alpha. There are plenty other weres here who could take my place."

"You have responsibilities."

"As do we all," Wolf said. "As do we all."

CHAPTER FIVE

I only love two people, even if they don't know it;
it's all I can afford.
~ Quin Kirkman, Journal

Laney set up a makeshift surgery in the women's dorm. She'd hung one of the worn blankets over the edge of the bunk, and told the vampire guard to wait on the other side. He stood, bemused, holding onto the packet of saline and bandages he had brought.

Laney was not fool enough to believe the vampire was harmless simply because his hands were full. He was humoring her for some unknown reason.

"Why do you need the blanket there?" the guard asked, seeming to stare at it, then her, then back at it.

"To provide privacy," Laney replied, her tone implying it was more than obvious.

"She has a bite on her neck that needs to be washed. I do not see why this requires privacy."

But he didn't pull the blanket down.

Laney leaned into the semi-dark space, now enclosed on three sides: one by blanket, two by concrete wall. She pulled the stained bandage from her sister's neck, dismayed to see the stream of blood running down from the bite. Vampires only needed to puncture the neck in two places then suck at the wound; Jane's neck was torn.

"Idiot," Laney muttered.

"Who is?" Jane asked, still as a stone.

"The vampire who bit you." She probably shouldn't have said that aloud, since a vampire stood nearby, but she couldn't contain herself.

The blanket swished to the side as the vampire guard leaned into their space. His eyes narrowed as he took in the wound, with its slowly congealing blood. He held out the saline and fresh bandage.

"You are correct in your assessment. This wound is unnecessary. I will speak with my superiors and ensure that the humans are fed from in an appropriate manner."

Jane turned to the guard. "Why do you care?"

Laney wanted to hush her, but it wasn't like she'd been particularly careful with her words, either. Instead, Laney tore open the small plastic saline tube and poured it onto the wound. She was careful to not use all of it. With one of the clean bandages, she wiped the wound as clean as possible, but that only made it renew bleeding. At least there weren't pieces of lint or anything stuck in the raw mess. Jane barely whimpered. Laney couldn't believe the tolerance for pain that Jane was exhibiting.

Her sister was truly amazing.

Laney then said the words she'd never imagined saying before: "Can you please lick the wound?"

Jane recoiled, giving Laney a look of betrayal.

The guard dropped the blanket and then walked around to stand next to Laney. Quite businesslike, he tilted Jane's head to the side and swept a long, glistening tongue over the wound. Laney watched critically, ignoring Jane's flinch and rapid breathing.

"Probably should do it again," she said.

Jane glared.

The guard repeated the process and then stood, licking his lips clean. His purple eyes bored into Jane's. "You taste sweet. That's probably why the vampire lost control. Warn whoever feeds next."

Like it was all Jane's fault. The asshole. But he was an asshole who had perhaps just saved Jane's life.

Nodding at Laney, the vampire turned on his heel and left, not even bothering to see if the wound began to heal. Placing a fresh bandage over the bite, Laney pressed down. Jane hissed.

"Hold this." Laney made Jane take hold of

the cloth. Turning around, she checked that no one was watching them. Quickly, she popped the contact from her eye and gave it a wash in the leftover saline solution. Then, she rinsed her eye with the liquid.

"Is anyone nearby?" Laney asked.

"No."

Sitting down next to Jane, facing the rear wall, Laney blinked rapidly, her eye singing with relief. Carefully, she held the contact in a small pool of water on her palm. It bobbed in time with the slight shaking of her hand, a brown striated circle with a clear center. She'd had to stockpile these a decade ago, rationing them out as long as she could. They were all well past their use-by, and she risked an eye infection wearing them, but she had to blend in with the humans. Her poor eye could do with more than a few minutes' break, but it was all she could risk. None of the other humans knew she was half-Graced. They'd hate her, maybe even hand her over to the weres or vampires for breeding purposes. Jane was luckier, because Hazel eyes didn't necessarily mean an active ability, and so the humans could tolerate her. But one fully colored eye? That was different.

After about five minutes, Laney popped the contact back into her eye. She'd long ago learned to do so without the aid of a mirror. Once righted, she turned back to her sister, who had been watching her silently.

"You made him *lick me*." The words had been

soft, but no less accusatory.

"We needed the saliva to help the wound heal," Laney said.

"But–"

"I know," Laney said. "I know."

♦

Laney knew it wouldn't be long before she was summoned to act as a donor. In the meantime, she had begun seeing to the small aches and pains and hurts of the female villagers. It gave her a purpose, and also strengthened the story she'd told about her being a doctor.

Doctors were expected to help people, after all.

Her makeshift surgery often meant poor Jane had to rest on the top bunk, as Laney had appropriated the bottom space, but her sister never complained. She knew that Laney needed something to do, or she'd go crazy. Back at the village, they'd at least had the veggie patch to worry over. Plus, each evening they had recited their research, gone over it, picked it apart. With Jane's memory, they hadn't even needed paper, which had long been unavailable. Here, they couldn't risk going over their work, and there was nothing else to do.

Her current patient was Maude, a forty-something woman who had recently fallen pregnant. She wouldn't say who the father was, and Laney didn't particularly care. She was doing a general checkup – the vampires thankfully hadn't fed from the woman yet – and everything seemed to be going fine. But she was limited in the things she could check. She'd asked the guards for more medical equipment, but most of them just ignored her requests. The first guard hadn't been back since.

Footsteps approached the shrouded bunk, but she ignored them. Pulling down the dull gray shirt over Maude's slightly protruding belly, she stood. "Everything seems to be tracking fine."

Maude made as if to stand, but the blanket was swished aside. A short female vampire stared at the both of them, her eyes lingering on the swell of Maude's stomach in a disconcerting manner.

Turning deep violet eyes on Laney, she pointed one finger at her. "You."

Laney looked at the finger. "Me?"

The vampire smiled, her teeth white and shiny in the light. "It's your turn."

CHAPTER SIX

I admire the were called Wolf. He's honest. Most of the time.
~ Quin Kirkman, Journal

Wolf could feel Trace's eyes on him as he stripped the arsenal of weapons from his body. Wolf's hands paused in their task. Looking up, he met the stern yellow gaze of his best friend and second in command. It was rare that two such strong alphas could get along as well as they did, but their friendship had been forged in a bloody childhood.

He went back to stripping away his weapons. If he was going to be captured, he didn't want to hand over his favorite knife, gun or garrote. Instead, he'd take fewer weapons of lesser quality. Enough not to raise questions, but not so numerous that he'd be losing too many of his clan's precious resources. Even though his teeth and claws were as deadly as any knife, there was a comfort he obtained from cold steel that he just couldn't get with his hands alone.

"This plan is foolhardy. It has so many holes in it, it's a joke." Trace's deep voice rumbled through the air.

"What else are we meant to do?"

Trace folded his arms across his mammoth chest. "Leave the humans to rot."

The werebear was being practical. Humans weren't people, at least, not anymore. Not since they became the only source of food available to his species.

Wolf glanced up from the pile of weapons spread over the metal table. They were in Wolf's room; it had a single bed, a desk, a chair and a shelf with a row of books. And now, a pile of weapons. "And potentially lose securing a Gray?"

"There will be other Graceds."

Wolf closed his eyes, his hands stilling. "Will there?"

Graceds were a dying breed; they owed nothing to humans and weres, or vampires. They'd experienced the worst suffering of all the humanoid species as a result of the centuries-long war. If it hadn't been for Quin's familial connection, they wouldn't even *have* the opportunity to permanently work with a Graced.

And in a way, Wolf felt like he owed Quin. Not him in particular, he figured, but the race as a whole. Wolf was second generation; his grandparents had been Graceds who'd been forced into being sperm and egg donors, and then his grandmothers into being gestational hosts. His parents had both been taken away from their mothers as soon as they were born and their yellow eyes became apparent. They'd then been held at separate laboratories until the activists had been foolish enough to break them free.

Funny how the activists had been some of the first to die.

That was the problem with raising someone in a cell; they didn't exactly have the best people skills. Both his parents had eventually figured out some semblance of civilization – mostly so they could fit in and pretend to be 'normal.' But the wildness had never really left them. How could it?

He couldn't have asked for better parents, though. They'd protected their pups with a fierceness that most humans couldn't imagine. All but two of their offspring were long dead though; only Wolf and his brother, Odo – Odolf – were left.

"We've held this stronghold for fifteen years; we'll hold it for another thousand if we have to," Trace said.

"I'm not concerned about the stronghold." They'd taken it through cunning and planning. They now knew every nook and cranny of the underground establishment; whoever tried to take it would be seriously underprepared. There was no way he was ever going to hand it back to a bunch of asshole vampires.

Wolf began selecting the weapons he had little attachment to and which could be – relatively – easily replaced. "I'm worried about the human settlements. If we lose those, we'll starve to death."

"We'll just put out more soldiers…"

"I don't even know why that settlement was left unprotected in the first place. It is well within our lands, but if anything, that means it should be *better* guarded. It was our own stupidity that did this. It's our job to set it right."

Wolf wasn't in charge of guard duty; he'd left that to a senior soldier who he'd thought was competent. He'd have a talk to the idiot and see why he'd decided that leaving a gaping big hole in their protection was suitable. They'd lost a handful of scouts and guards when the vampires had breached the perimeter, but the leeches had done it so fast and so cleanly that it took Quin informing them of the infiltration for them to learn of it.

Whoever had done the genetic engineering to ensure that weres and vampires could only survive on human flesh and human blood had been an absolute moron. They'd probably planned to create the necessary organs in a bunch of petri dishes, to be doled out as needed. But when the labs were destroyed, so too was that handy renewable resource. Now, the clan's doctor (the only one they had) had to harvest livers from humans – cut away just enough so that the liver could grow back on its own, but also enough so that whoever fed off it would be sustained. Then hope the human didn't die from infection. It was a massive flaw in their system. If they could survive off cow or sheep or any other kind of liver, then they wouldn't need to be tied to an ever-dwindling human population.

They'd be free.

"Security has been increased," Trace said. "I talked to the soldier who'd been in charge of the roster and deployment."

"Can they still walk?" Wolf raised an eyebrow.

"For now."

Trace had probably kept his temper in check, then. The man was lethal when riled; it was part of his bear nature. While the soldier *was* at fault, there were only a few hundred weres in the clan, and they had to patrol an area of several hundred acres. Mistakes could – and did – happen because of short-staffing.

"We should seriously start considering bringing the humans closer in, maybe even housing them in the bunker," Wolf said, sliding a hunting knife into a sheath and strapping it to his thigh.

It's what the vampires often did. Kept the food source straight at hand. But the weres believed that humans needed sunshine and fresh air to be healthy; and the healthier the human, the quicker they'd grow their liver back.

"There isn't room for all of them in the bunker."

Which was true, unfortunately. But they had to be better able to protect their food source. Not all of them were wolves; there were bears, coyotes, and a couple of leopards, although it was hard for the cat shifters and wolves to live under the same roof. Their animal sides bristled, while the human halves tried to get along. But they all had one thing in common: the need to eat.

CHAPTER SEVEN

I've stolen so many medical supplies over my life.
Maybe that should be on my tombstone: 'Here lies
Quin, scary son-of-a-bitch and stealer of saline
solution.' (My favorite is the SOB part.)
~ Quin Kirkman, Journal

Laney was taken from the dormitory and led down a series of halls. She was with a group of five other women, who were joined by six of the men from the settlement. She recognized all of their faces, knew them all by name, but somehow they felt like strangers. They were all quiet, some with expressions of fear, others with faces strangely blank. She couldn't see any bite marks on any of their necks, which were left exposed by the low-necked shirts and sweaters they had been provided. They emerged through a steel door and into the weak sunshine, the sky a washed-out blue. It had once been a bright

color, she was told; a shade of azure so intense
it could sing in the soul. Now, that hue could
only be seen in the eyes of a Graced.

Laney took a deep breath of the air, but the
smell of chemicals, feces and metal reached her.
She hadn't had a clean breath of air in too long
to remember. At least it had been better at the
were settlement. The gravel-laden ground
crunched under her feet as she came to a stop.

"This way," the female guard barked.

Laney wished that the guards wore name
badges. It would help keep them straight in her
mind, rather than 'Scary Vampire 1' and so on.
Although, it was probably better she didn't
know. She'd start to humanize the creatures in
her mind if she knew their names. While they
looked human, they were far from it. She had to
remember that.

The woman, along with a male guard,
herded the small group across the gravel
toward a large building that stood proudly,
made entirely of steel, by what she could see.
They entered through a side door, which the
female guard held open. She bared her fangs as
the prisoners walked by her, snapping her teeth
at Melanie, who flinched on her way past. *Show
no fear*, she told herself. Building her courage,
Laney settled a glare on the vampire, who
winked at her.

"Adrenaline makes the blood taste better,"
the guard said.

Once inside, they were led down another

series of corridors and into a main dining hall. Laney updated her mental map as they went. She'd always had an excellent sense of direction; she thought it might be something to do with being part-Gray. Quin seemed to have the same ability.

Once they were all inside the room, the female vampire indicated they should line up in a single row. There was a little jostling as they got into place, but they were eerily silent as they did so. Laney couldn't stop the little shiver that ran through her.

Looking out over the room, Laney studied the mostly empty expanse. There was a single table that ran across the middle – twenty chairs stood in position on either side, with one at the head. They were all vacant. The table was decorated with pitchers of water and some fruit and meat. Laney wasn't sure why the food was there; vampires could eat human nourishment, but they received most of their sustenance from blood. Maybe it was for the humans after they had been drunk from? It certainly looked more appealing than the gruel she'd been eating until now.

At some unspoken signal, the vampire guards stood tall and alert in a military resting stance: feet apart and arms behind their back. Seconds later, a door at the rear of the room swung open and a line of vampires flowed in. At their head was a short man with dark curly hair; he was followed by a woman with deep brown skin and bleached white locks. Then another ten vampires followed. They were dressed in various styles of clothing, but their attire wasn't costly like she'd assumed it would be. A couple even wore guard uniforms. The last to enter was a statuesque woman with long auburn hair tied into a braid. Her violet eyes were wide in her face; almost too large. Her chin was sharp and pointed, her cheekbones high. She was stunningly beautiful, but there was something about her that was utterly alien. Maybe it was the smoothness of movement, the wide unblinking stare that made her seem like something truly *other*.

The auburn-haired vampire moved to the head of the table and took a seat. The other vampires, who'd each come to stand behind a chair, followed suit. She waved a hand languidly at the line of humans, her gaze scanning them. Laney's eyes tracked the movement, locking on the delicate-seeming forearm. A line of numbers marched across the inside of the wrist and next to it, a tattoo of a raven.

The digits represented her serial number, which meant the vampire was first generation. And...the raven tattoo only belonged to one member of that prestigious group. This was Tatiana Romanov.

Laney took a few quick shallow breaths, trying not to let her panic show. Tatiana. Bloody. Romanov. They were screwed. There was no way Quin would be able to break her and Jane out from this facility. They were as good as blood slaves for the rest of their lives. Tatiana was known to lead the most vicious of all vampire groups. Even she'd heard the rumors. Why hadn't Jane mentioned this? Laney could understand the others not recalling, as they would have been affected by the saliva, but surely her sister would have noticed. Jane noticed *everything*.

"Before we partake of this much deserved meal," Tatiana began, her voice low and level, "we have an issue to address." She reclined back in her chair, the picture of ease and relaxation.

There was a subtle tensing at the table.

Tatiana gave the vampires a genial smile, ignoring the humans lined up before them. "I believe that someone at this table has been remiss during their feedings."

The room was so quiet that Laney could hear her own heartbeat pounding in her ears. She should probably keep her gaze on the ground, like the woman next to her, but she couldn't look away.

Those large violet eyes skimmed over the vampires. "Would anyone know anything about that?"

Silence.

A sound, loud as a gunshot, ricocheted through the room. So quickly Laney hadn't been able to follow, Tatiana had slammed her fist into the steel table. The metal had buckled under the impact. Three pitchers lay upturned, trickling puddles of water across the table; in one case, onto a vampire's lap. The dark-skinned man didn't move, frozen in place as liquid spilled over his legs.

"Does *anyone* know *anything* about this?" Tatiana's voice rose and fell in pitch, her face almost feral.

Suddenly, Tatiana was in front of Laney, the woman having moved so fast she was a blur. A finger jabbed the air in front of her face, the digit tipped with a sharp nail. "You!"

Laney blinked. Her heart started to pound even louder. "Me?"

"Did you have to patch up another human because of a bite that would not heal?" Tatiana's expression was almost manic.

"I–"

Tatiana tapped Laney on the forehead. Hard.

Laney bit back the flinch, and took a deep breath.

"Come on, use your brain. I am assured humans have one. Did you, or did you not, have to patch up a human due to a mangled bite?"

The guard who had helped her that day wasn't in the room, but she assumed he'd been the one who tattled. She hadn't really thought that far ahead.

"Y-Yes." She hadn't meant to stammer, but when you had one of the oldest people in the world staring at you with a crazed glint in her eye...

Finally, one of the other vampires spoke. She was a short, curvy woman with midnight dark hair and jet black skin. "Please provide more detail as to the description of 'mangled.'"

Tatiana's head whipped around, quick as a snake, but while she glared, she didn't tell the other woman to shut up. Even while staring at the other vampire, she barked, "Speak." Laney assumed it was directed at her.

"I noticed that a bite was not healing on one of the other villagers." Best to keep the familial relation out of the story, Laney thought. "I inspected the wound and realized it was not two clean puncture marks, but more of a gash. I asked for medical supplies to clean the sore, to prevent infection. The wound was also not healing at the expected rate; there did not appear to have been a liberal enough application of saliva."

"What would you know about vampire bites?" This was from a different vampire. The first one to enter the room.

She felt the attention of all the vampires lock on her. Some of them stared at her throat. "I am – was – a doctor."

"Little young, don't you think?" The man's voice was taunting.

"As if you can tell the age of a human; they all look the same." That quip was from the bleached blonde.

"I graduated early, top of my class. I then went on to obtain further qualifications in immunology and genetic manipulation."

The bleached blonde bared her teeth. "Not much use for either of those fields now, is there?"

Laney narrowed her eyes at the speaker.

"We all know how much I love a geneticist," this was from Tatiana, "but since you are too young to have been involved in my...development...you can live."

Laney gulped. She had a feeling that Tatiana had been utterly serious. "Thank you?"

Tatiana tilted her head in acknowledgment, magnanimous.

"Would the human have died if you had not helped her?"

"She was at risk of an infection, which without antibiotics, it could have killed her. Yes."

"So not an immediate risk?"

"No, but people's mouths contain a lot of bacteria, even vampires. Vampire saliva itself isn't harmful, but it also contains an antibacterial property that neutralizes the other contaminants. If it is not applied, then it doesn't clean the wound. There was a high risk of infection."

"So, according to this *human*, someone here foolishly risked the life of one of our blood donors." Tatiana spun back to face the table and its occupants. "There are some basic facts to our existence. We drink blood. We lick the wound clean. We get the human *to heal. We can't drink from dead humans!"* Tatiana was screaming the last sentence, her face contorted with rage.

"Are you all idiots? We're fighting a war and you're too busy goring humans to think properly? Is that it?"

Tatiana strode forward, grabbing the man who had taunted Laney by the back of the neck. She plucked him up, knocking the chair to the ground. His legs kicked the air, and he twisted, trying to break loose.

With a flick of the wrist, she snapped his neck, paralyzing him. His limbs drooped, like a puppet with its strings cut. The sheer strength it took…no human could have done something like that. Even most *vampires* couldn't.

"If you are going to behave like animals, then you will be treated as such. Is this clear?" Tatiana looked at each vampire before she opened her mouth, her fangs glistening. Then she sank her teeth into the vampire's throat. She began to drink, long gulps, before she ripped her teeth away, leaving a pulsing wound that spouted into the air. Laney took an instinctive step back toward the wall.

She hadn't realized that vampires could drink from one another.

Blood dripped in a crimson stream down Tatiana's lips and chin. With her free hand, she punched it through the vampire's torso, pulling out his heart. Dropping the body on the ground, Tatiana took a bite out of the stuttering organ, chewing slowly.

"Let this be a lesson," she said through a mouthful of flesh. "Risk the lives of our *only food source* and you will become the food. Is this clear?"

CHAPTER EIGHT

Everyone thinks they're infallible, but they're wrong. Except for me. I'm awesome.
~ Quin Kirkman, Journal

How had these vampire idiots ever managed to sneak onto were land and steal all those humans from under his nose? He'd been in their clan boundary for well over an hour and he hadn't heard a single peep from the local leeches. Their security was terrible. Either they didn't know he was there, or they were watching him to see what he'd do.

He had a feeling it was the former.

Wolf hadn't spotted any security cameras – they were pretty rare now, so he doubted they'd be placed out in the border woodlands – and only a handful of guards. That would have been fine, had the guards not completely missed the fact a werewolf was patrolling their lands.

He was going to have to have a chat to his soldiers when he returned. If this was how his people patrolled, heads were going to roll. Literally.

Staying crouched, Wolf gently pushed aside the fronds of a half-dead fern. Peering out past the small shrubs that concealed him, he looked over the large fence that guarded the compound behind it. Shaking his head, he couldn't believe he'd gotten so close. Scaling the fence and getting in would be a lot harder to do undetected, but that was okay, since he planned on getting caught anyway.

The oaks either side of him were tall and sturdy, which meant that this compound was probably a hundred years old. The large metal warehouses that ringed three sides of an open expanse had rust stains on their roofs, but they otherwise seemed to be in good condition. The courtyard was just packed dirt and gravel, not even concrete. No humans were visible, but Wolf would bet his eye teeth that the compound had underground levels. Most of these places did, back when bombs were dropped without too much thought to the consequences. The humans would either be there, or in one of the warehouses.

It was only when the humans had fled to rural areas, or congregated in the last few intact cities, that the vampires – and weres, he grudgingly admitted – had realized what had happened. And then they'd started gathering their food supplies closer to their chests. Destroying those who fought back. Culling the smart ones, leaving only the stupid to breed.

Tilting his chin up, Wolf sniffed the air. The icy stink of vampires was strong, filtering through the small breeze to reach his hiding place. There was a hint of human there as well, and the cloying sweet stench of death. Someone had died recently. He hoped it wasn't one of Quin's sisters. That would make this job a lot more difficult; Wolf doubted he could pass one human off for another. He could picture the interaction now.

"No, Quin, *this* girl is your sister."

Quin's look of disbelief, and then a narrowing of dangerous Gray eyes. The compound collapsing because of an internal earthquake.

There was a reason the Grays were one of the most feared of the Graceds. Sure, a Green could know what you were thinking, unless you were another Green or had a handy natural mental shield like Wolf did. But you could lie to yourself or try to cloak your thoughts, to avoid having a Green listen to your mind. You could do nothing to a person who could break your neck without even having to be in the same room as you. Grays may not have the super speed of a vampire or were, or the strength, but they didn't need it.

Now, Wolf thought, it was time to go get caught.

Sniffing the air, Wolf detected the nearest vampire guard. Moving closer to them, he stood upwind, so his scent would wash down to them. He saw the moment the vampire realized there was a were nearby. The man's violet eyes widened, and he grabbed the handle of the gun that was belted to his waist.

Right, because a gun was going to be useful when fighting a were, Wolf thought.

Wolf made sure he broke a few conspicuous branches as he moved closer to the compound.

"Omega to Raven, we have a were near the perimeter of the compound."

Wolf paused. They still had radios. That was cool. He'd have to try and steal some when he broke out.

"Raven to Omega. Seize the were. Bring it in alive if possible."

Wolf stalked the vampire. He saw the leech swivel around as he finally registered that the were was a lot closer than he thought. Whipping out the gun, the vampire spotted Wolf through the trees and let off a shot.

Wolf dodged, dropping down low and running through the bush. Automatically, his feet flew over roots and brambles as he headed back toward the boundary line. It's what he would do if he weren't trying to get caught, after all. Another few gunshots sounded, and Wolf felt one thud into his side. He would have laughed at the idiocy of shooting a were with nothing more than a toy, but a burning sensation started crawling up through the wound.

Silver.

Wolf felt two more thuds, and then his knees locked up, refusing to work. Normally, a silver bullet alone wouldn't stop him for long, allergy or not. But something was wrong. Panting, lying face-first in the dirt, Wolf tried to prop himself up on his arms, but they were weak, as if he were nothing more than a newborn pup.

Two sets of booted feet came into his line of sight.

"Thought you could run away, fleabag?"

One of the boots moved, and Wolf tried to roll out of the way. He only partially succeeded, and was kicked brutally in the shoulder as a result. At least it hadn't been his head.

"They wanted him *alive*," a second voice spoke.

"But they didn't say conscious."

CHAPTER NINE

Sometimes vampires just gross me out. Did you ever hear about that time Tatiana ate a guy's face off? No, well you have now.
~ Quin Kirkman, Journal

Tatiana dropped the partially eaten heart on the body of the broken vampire and wiped her hands on her pants, as if dusting off a day's work in the fields. The vampires all stared at her from their seated positions, but each one nodded when Tatiana's eyes met theirs.

Laney could hardly breathe.

The woman had just ripped a man's heart *from his chest* and eaten it. Raw. Right there in front of everyone.

"Now!" Tatiana clapped her hands together and smiled, her teeth white in her blood-smeared face. "It's time to eat." Her voice was almost singsong.

Laney couldn't stop the fine tremors that had started all over her body. She didn't want to end up like the vampire on the floor, but she didn't think she could tolerate being fed from. She'd been prepared to fake the high that came with vampire saliva, but she wasn't sure she could, not after everything she'd just witnessed. Sure, Laney was a doctor and had seen hearts before. But she hadn't watched them being chewed and swallowed.

Tatiana swung around to stare at the line of humans. Laney wished she could shrink back and become invisible, but she had a feeling she'd already made herself unforgettable, at least for tonight.

One by one, the vampires stood and stared at the humans. Tatiana waved a languid hand and the guards shuffled the line of humans forward. As Laney approached the table, she couldn't keep her eyes from drifting to the discarded body, which was being ignored as if it didn't exist by the other vampires. Maybe things like this happened all the time, who knew?

Laney certainly hoped that she wouldn't find out if it was a regular occurrence.

Tatiana held up a hand as Laney walked by the auburn-haired vampire. "Not you."

Laney froze, eyes locked on the hand. It was covered in gore. *Look down*, an inner voice whispered. *You don't want her to notice your contact lens.* Most humans only saw it if they stared long enough, but someone with Tatiana's vision would detect it in seconds if Laney wasn't careful.

"Not me?" Laney felt her eyebrows rise.

"You have done me a service already these last few days. I hear you have been assisting the other cattle in the warehouse. And you potentially saved the life of an individual feeder. I value all contributions to my clan. Plus," she motioned at the body on the floor, "there is one less mouth to feed."

"T-Thank you."

Tatiana nodded and Laney backed away to stand back at the wall. She could feel the eyes of the other humans in the room, some angry, some jealous, some just blank. Somehow though, it was worse watching all the others become dinner for the vampires; seeing the vampires extend their fangs, watching the moment of panic skitter across the humans' faces, then witnessing the euphoria dance across their features as the vampire saliva hit their bloodstream.

Laney felt rather like a voyeur, observing something she shouldn't be witness to. Three of the vampires dropped back from their 'cattle,' lips glistening red in the dim light. They reminded her of sated ticks.

A vampire guard ran into the room then, his black uniform in contrast to the pure white of his skin. He almost looked like an albino, which made Laney narrow her eyes. As far as she was aware, albinos had an instant death sentence nowadays.   Apparently   something malfunctioned in their genetic makeup, making them unstable and dangerous. She didn't know how truthful that was, considering she'd never met one, or been able to study them. But when she caught the vampire's gaze, it was a purple so pale as to be almost gray.

"Lady Tatiana," the guard said. From Laney's position, she could unfortunately see and hear everything with clarity. She didn't think she'd forget those slurping sounds anytime soon.

The vampire raised an irritated face from her food's neck. With an internal wince, Laney realized it was Melanie. The poor girl was terrified of her own shadow, let alone vampires or weres. Laney couldn't see her face, but she hoped the drug-laced saliva was doing its thing.

"There had better be a good reason for this interruption. I have already had a trying evening."

Laney noted with amazement that the guard's attention did not stray from Tatiana. Surely he could smell the dead body in the room?

"Our guards just captured a were."

CHAPTER TEN

*Sometimes – heck, most of the time – pretending
that you're less than you are is the only way to stay
alive.*
~ Quin Kirkman, Journal

Wolf was being dragged down a corridor. They
could have put him on a stretcher, but that
would make taking the stairs far less
entertaining for them. Each time they hauled
him down a flight, he couldn't stop his face or
body from contorting in agony. It felt as if
someone had poured acid into the three gunshot
wounds; acid which was slowly spreading
through his veins. When had these bloody
leeches developed such a weapon? It had to be
soluble silver or something.

Either way, it hurt like nothing he'd ever
experienced before. And he thought he'd been
familiar with pain.

Wolf tried to pay attention to his surroundings, but he could barely keep his eyes open. Finally, his captors dumped him in a cold concrete room. He figured he was probably a hundred yards underground. When he could finally open his eyes and *think*, he'd be able to confirm his suspicions.

Someone kicked him savagely in the side, and he didn't bother to choke back the growl that rose from his chest.

"Looks like we bagged some sort of dog," one of the vampires said. He didn't recognize the voice as the one who captured him. The leech had a different stench about him as well. Great, he'd been so out of it he hadn't even realized they'd swapped guards.

"Shame, I rather wished he was a cat or something. Be more fun to play with." That came from a female.

Maybe he should open his eyes and check his surroundings, but now his ribs hurt as well as all the other wounds. At least the ribs should heal on their own, quickly, provided that the silver in the ammunition didn't interfere.

He heard the air move as someone squatted down next to him. The sweet, cloying aroma of icy blood reached his nostrils. At least his sense of smell was still working. "I sure hope you enjoy a good wrestling match, 'cause I'm keen to taste some doggy blood." The voice was husky and feminine.

Wolf bared his teeth in reply.

The vampire laughed, and he heard them leave, the door shutting behind him with an ominous click. Silence descended and he rolled onto his back, the cool concrete a relief against his boiling blood. As he tried to relax against the pain, he opened his eyes. As he suspected, he was lying on the ground in a concrete cell. There was a metal frame for a bed next to him, but there wasn't a mattress on it, only metal slats.

A bucket of water stood in one corner, a steel toilet next to it. Nice standards of hygiene there. He sniffed the air, and scented the cold stench of disuse, along with a more recent odor of vampire blood. Someone else was trapped down here with him. The icy smell of vampires permeated the area; so the guards had been coming in and out of here pretty frequently, he guessed.

"So, they brought me a fleabag for company." The words were raspy and hoarse, like the owner hadn't spoken for a while; only screamed. Wolf guessed his prison mate was a leech. Weres didn't tend to call each other fleabags. And he doubted a human would be kept down here.

Wolf thought about sitting up, but he didn't have the energy. Suddenly, the plan that had seemed somewhat foolproof had become less likely to succeed. Not unless this silver poisoning was over quickly, and he wasn't dead at the end of it.

"Lucky me, I have a leech for company."

Wolf's response was roughened with pain.

"What's your name?" the other prisoner asked.

"John. John Smith," Wolf said. It was a bit of an old joke. Only someone who'd been around back when humans had been plentiful would recognize it.

A snort reached his ears. "And I'm Tatiana Romanov."

Wolf grunted. "I'd have to kill you if you were."

The vampire barked a sound between a laugh and a groan. "You'd have to get in line."

CHAPTER ELEVEN

I used to wonder why I could level cities when my sister could barely throw someone across a room. Then I realized we had different talents.
~ Quin Kirkman, Journal

"What do you know about vampire physiology?"

Laney's spine locked at the low words spoken next to her ear. She hadn't even heard the speaker approach. Turning her head on the side, from where she'd been staring at the ceiling in her bunk bed, she met the purple gaze of the guard who had reluctantly helped her. Scary Vampire 1, she named him, or SV1.

"The basics," Laney replied. She wasn't about to tell him her expertise had been in werewolf and vampire biology.

"Come with me."

Laney didn't bother to argue. Over the past

week, she'd learned to keep her head down and only bother the guards when it came to the other humans' welfare. It meant that they gave her a grudging respect, and strangely, that they didn't bring her in for feeding. It was as if she did a service for them, so they left her alone in payment. Laney was worried that the situation could change at any moment.

And that moment may have come.

Jumping down from the bunk, she followed SV1 out of the room, casting a quick look over her shoulder at Jane. Her sister's eyes were wide, but she kept her lips sealed. The guard didn't look back to see if Laney followed, but she figured he could hear her keeping up.

After they left the dormitory room, the guard turned to her. "If you talk to *anyone* about what you're going to see, your life is forfeit. Food source or no food source. Tatiana's orders."

Laney just watched him.

"Anyone includes your sister. And whoever you tell, they're dead, too."

"I get it."

He nodded and then turned back around.

They soon turned left and went down a corridor Laney hadn't seen before. Halfway down the hall there was a door; it stood closed and forbidding with a 'do not enter' sign. In her youth, she might have taken that as a challenge. Nowadays, she just wanted to avoid anything that screamed unnecessary danger.

The guard moved to the door and opened it.

He beckoned for her to follow.

Great.

Not that the death threat hadn't hinted that something bad was afoot. As they walked down the five flights of stairs, Laney was thankful for the regular physical work she'd done on the farms near the settlement. If she'd been kept by the weres like the vampires kept their cattle, she'd be struggling to get down the stairs, let alone back up them again.

When they reached the bottom, Laney tried not to visibly look around, but SV1 wasn't paying attention to her. There were ten cells in the area; each one had metal bars across its front and concrete sides, ceiling and floor. It looked more like an old-fashioned jail than a prison for vampires or weres. Maybe that is what it used to be.

Only two cells were occupied.

One at the far right end had a man who was lying on the concrete floor, his limbs akimbo. The cell two doors down from that one had another figure in it. This one was lying on the metal bed that was in the room. It had a thin mattress of foam, which didn't seem to do much to support the supine form.

"This one." SV1 pointed at the figure on the bed. He unlocked the door and motioned her inside. "We need to keep him alive."

Laney's eyes grew wide as she took in the full impact of the sight before her. The man was a vampire, but he was skin and bones. He wore a worn pair of combat pants and nothing else. Three wooden stakes protruded from his torso; scabs had formed around them. Wide eyes stared at the guard then her.

"Traitor," the man spat. Blood dribbled down his chin.

The guard ignored him. "How do we preserve the prisoner's life?"

Laney couldn't keep the retort back. "Well, I'd start by pulling out the stakes."

The guard turned to her, expression blank. "Tatiana wants him tortured."

Laney took a few steps forward, staring down at the figure. She had no medical equipment with her, but then, what was she to do? Take some blood samples, all of which would show that the vampire had IgE in their system; that they were suffering an allergic reaction to the wood? The man had wooden stakes embedded in his abdomen, although none next to his heart, since that would have already ended him. But the wounds surrounding the stakes were swollen and inflamed and an angry red. Spreading out from the impact wound were lines of raised welts, fading into a rash.

"If you want him to live, then you need to remove the stakes. I'd recommend injecting him with some adrenaline, if you have any." While vampire immune systems were able to heal most injuries quickly, wood inhibited that ability. The allergens would have interacted with his bloodstream, and if left unchecked, would eventually cause internal heart failure that even a vampire's system couldn't fix.

"How long will it take to heal?"

Laney shut her eyes. She'd said she only had a basic understanding of vampire biology. Any concrete answers would give away her lie. "I'm not sure. I'd need to clean the wound, make sure no lingering traces of wood are present. If you don't have adrenaline or an antihistamine, it could take longer to heal." She doubted that any of the less common medications like glucocorticoids would be readily available. Plus, they'd have to be calibrated to the vampire immune system.

"Do you need more saline and cloths?" the guard asked.

A barking laugh emerged from the other cell. "A bit of water and some material will surely heal some stake wounds." The words were deep, almost gravelly. For some reason, a shiver wound down her spine at their sound.

"Did I ask your opinion, puppy?" That emerged from her soon-to-be patient.

"Puppy? I can't wait to rip your throat out." It was said almost cheerfully.

"I can't wait for you to try."

Laney ignored the strange banter. "Don't you have any doctors here?" she asked the guard.

SV1's eyes locked on her. "Vampires don't generally need medical assistance."

Right.

"Step out of the cell," SV1 said.

Laney did as she was told. The vampire locked the door and then eyed the remaining cells. "Wait here, and I'll get you the supplies we have. Don't step too close to the cells. These prisoners are dangerous, even if they don't appear it."

CHAPTER TWELVE

I've never really contemplated a happy ending, not for myself. But I do hope my sisters will find joy, somehow. I've yet to work that part out.
~ Quin Kirkman, Journal

"Aww, did the guard just show the little human concern?" Wolf couldn't help the taunt that emerged. He'd been stuck down in the cell for days, his wounds spreading fire through his body. It hadn't led to an improved temperament. It would also be another three days before Trace would send a party to come looking for him. Trace and Quin had given Wolf a week to try and break the girls out, or they – more accurately, *Quin* – were coming to get them instead.

"I guess he doesn't want the only doctor eaten." That was from the human. The statement was so dry it made him thirsty. Quin hadn't mentioned that the vampires had access to a human doctor when he'd given his intel.

"Maybe you could come and check me out, then." If he hadn't been in so much pain, and the human was close enough to see his face, he might have waggled his eyebrows.

"Aside from the obvious, is there anything wrong with you?"

"What do you mean by 'obvious'?"

"Well, you're certainly a little unhinged. But I'm not a psychiatrist, so that's just conjecture."

"I doubt there are any left. I reckon they would have been all eaten." He heard the vampire chuckle-wheeze at his statement.

"Yeah, they would have been some of the first on the list," the vampire said. "Aside from the geneticists. All that 'how do you *feel*' bullshit, or the 'was killing that person *really* necessary?' was annoying."

He thought he heard the human gulp.

"When did the clan get a doctor, anyway?" That was from the vampire.

"I was taken in the last raid," the human spoke slowly.

Quin – or Trace – hadn't mentioned there were any human doctors in the village. How little did they even know about their cattle? If there'd been a doctor, then he'd have had them moved into the compound; they needed every potential surgeon they could get their hands on. The precise removal of livers meant that the humans could survive the harvest; it was important it was done right. He had some weres who were trained to do the extraction, but only one dedicated to the task. Sometimes were instincts would kick in and things would end rather badly.

Wolf heard the vampire guard's footsteps approach the prison area and decided to bite back on the last retort. Instead, he lay on the floor quietly. He'd decided it was a more comfortable option compared to the metal slats of the bed. His prison mate's identity had yet to be confirmed, but he had a suspicion as to who he was spending his jail time with.

He wondered why Tatiana hadn't just killed Marcus outright. It's what Wolf would have done, if he forcibly took over another were's territory. It was foolish to leave your enemies alive.

"Here," he heard the vampire guard say. The sound of a door unlocking and footsteps echoed throughout the concrete rooms.

"I need to pull the stakes out." The human sounded confident, authoritative even. Which wasn't expected. He'd thought that most humans were gutless. It came with being thought of as food by pretty much everything else.

He wished he could see her face. He didn't know why, but something within him was curious to know what she looked like. It was stupid of him. Humans couldn't be thought of as more than food, no matter how handy or intelligent they may be. Yet her voice was melting his insides each time he heard it. Or maybe it was just the acid-pain of the silver poison. Now, she was murmuring to the guard and vampire in the other cell. A muted yell emerged, and Wolf figured that one of the stakes had been pulled.

"Come on," Wolf yelled. "Don't be weak. Oh, wait. You're a leech. Keep screaming like the soft-cock you really are."

A few panting breaths, then, "Fuck. You."

Wolf hated to admit it, but he felt sorry for the vampire – Marcus. To be deposed and then kept alive for torture. There was no honor in that. Wolf would've ripped out the man's throat and been done with it.

He listened as the vampire was given a thorough once-over. It did sound like she was continuing the torture rather effectively for Tatiana, with the vampire's grunts and moans, but eventually the room grew quiet.

"He's passed out," the human said. Wolf rolled his head to one side, listening.

"Weak."

"His body partially healed around the stake. I'd say he showed remarkable strength to keep conscious as long as he did."

A snort.

"There, I've finished."

CHAPTER THIRTEEN

I had a meeting with Gemma Frost yesterday. She's one of the most powerful Greens I've ever met, and she's fifteen. In the last generation, there have been four Greens born who are so powerful, they have to live mostly in isolation. There are only a dozen people on the continent whose thoughts remain private from their powerful minds. I think it's a sign of things to come.
~ Quin Kirkman, Journal

Laney took a deep breath and stripped the latex gloves from her hands. Thankfully, the guard had brought a few extra supplies with him when he returned. No adrenaline, alas. The vampire prisoner was unconscious, but she wasn't sure how long he'd stay like that. The internal damage and inflammation caused by the stakes had been severe, so it was probably for his own good that his body had given out.

"While we're here, you may as well check out the other prisoner." As the guard helped gather the supplies back together, he cast a sneer at the other vampire. Laney decided she didn't want to know what the injured vampire had done to deserve being tortured.

Opening a bag, she shoved the used gauze and gloves into it. "What's one more patient?"

She was already in so far over her head it wasn't a joke.

SV1 walked to the unconscious vampire's cell door and opened it, motioning for her to go through. He then locked it, before taking the ten steps to the other cell. "This one isn't a vampire."

Laney raised an eyebrow and followed the guard inside. She'd gathered as much from the 'puppy' comment. Her eyes widened as she got a clear look at the man on the floor. Even with a face covered in bruises, his clothes torn in so many places they didn't serve much as covering, he was still the most handsome man she'd ever laid eyes on. He had blond-brown dreadlocks, which were tied back in a ponytail, and a face that was so perfectly proportioned it should be illegal. Strong jaw, aquiline nose, bright yellow eyes…

She shook herself, hoping the vampire hadn't picked up on her daydreaming. *That's great, very professional,* she told herself. Eyeing off a patient as if he was a potential breeding partner. He was a *were*; there was no way she was going to be doing any kind of breeding with him.

"What happened to him?" She didn't see any silver stakes jutting from his chest. Leaning forward, she noted patches of dried blood on his shirt and trousers. The blood surrounded three small holes.

Those bright eyes stared up at her. "I was shot, princess."

Fighting the urge to take a step back, she knelt down on the concrete floor instead. The cold seeped into her knees.

"Shot with what?" Laney turned to look up at the guard, who folded his arms across his chest and appeared bored.

"Bullets." That was from the were.

"Then you just need them removed? Why do I need to do that? Couldn't anyone? I'm sure you all have a lot of practice at it by now." She probably shouldn't be so sarcastic, but really, in for a penny...

The were glowered at SV1. "They weren't normal bullets, were they, leech-boy?"

Frowning, Laney leaned forward and began inspecting the wounds, ripping his shirt away for one of them. He hissed as she tore away dried blood. Angry lines striated outward from the impact points, where the skin had darkened to a tainted blue-black. She noticed that his muscled chest was moving up and down quickly – he was breathing faster than he needed to. And his skin was warm to touch; warmer than it probably should be. His skin was surprisingly smooth, without as much hair as she'd expect from a were…

You're losing it, she scolded herself. *Temperature. That's what you need to focus on.* Though without a thermometer, she couldn't be sure if he had a fever. Sweat glistened on his skin, despite the cool of the room. It was almost like the wounds had gone septic. In addition, necrotic tissue had formed near the entry holes in two of the three wounds. The allergic reaction had gone critical in those locations. She figured his internal organs could be in just as poor condition. And his heart, that might not last much longer, depending on how much silver had entered the bloodstream.

"What was in those bullets?" Laney leaned back on her heels and looked up at the guard.

The vampire was silent for long moments. "Silver nitrate."

Laney sighed. "Which dissolves in water."

Even weres were about sixty percent water.

She didn't know how to counteract silver poisoning in weres; not when it was in the bloodstream itself. If it was a stake or a bullet, she could pull it out. But this wouldn't be so simple.

"What does it feel like?" Laney asked the were, looking at his forehead rather than meeting his sharp gaze. Even prostrate on the ground with silver poisoning, he was horribly alert.

The were lay there, panting, a wheeze

present under the heavy breaths, not saying anything for long moments. She didn't think he'd answer. "Like acid being poured through my veins."

The guard shifted his stance.

"Keep the excitement down," the were said, looking at the vampire with a sneer. "I'm trying to die peacefully here."

"Can you help him or not?" the guard asked Laney.

She stared at the wounds, noticing how the blue-black color was beginning to spread over his skin, radiating from the wound. "I honestly don't know. You'd need to get the silver out; so you'd have to bleed him, since it's in his blood. But then he'd need a human liver to replenish his stores…"

"I need to consult with Tatiana. Do you think he's much of a threat?"

Laney wasn't sure. He was a were; injured as he was…

"Possibly."

"Then stay out of arm's reach."

The guard left, locking her in the cell with the were. Eyes wide, she stared openmouthed as the guard disappeared up the stairs. Quickly, she jumped to her feet, scrambling away until her back was pressed against the bars. They felt like brands of ice against her heated skin.

"A little trusting, don't you think?" the were asked her.

"Yes."

"Is the vampire still unconscious?"

Laney peered through the cell bars, careful to angle her body as far away from him as possible. "It looks like it." It was hard to see, but the figure was as she'd left him, lying on the bed, arms folded across his chest, like a corpse.

Before she could blink, the were had rolled onto his side and come to stand before her.

Laney pressed herself further against the bars, heart pounding. She was an idiot…a fool…

The were toppled forward, landing completely against her. All his smooth planes and rock hard muscles pressed into her. Her heart began to pound for a different reason. Using one arm, he propped himself away from her. "Sorry about that. Weaker than I thought."

Laney tried to lean further away. Her body was stupid, stupid. Why was it reacting to something like *him*? *Now*?

Suddenly, she felt him nuzzling her throat. Was he *sniffing* her?

"You smell nice. Why do you smell nice? You're cattle."

She had to try and get control of the situation before the guard came back. But her brain wasn't working properly. "This isn't creepy at all."

The were drew back with a jerk, and nearly fell over. Laney reached out and grabbed one of his arms. She felt herself squeezing the muscle without permission from her brain. Thankfully, he didn't seem to register what her hand was doing. She let go.

He lowered his voice, until she felt it almost reverberating within her. "I'm here looking for two girls."

Her mind went blank. "Two girls?"

"Humans from one of m—our settlements were just stolen. I'm trying to track down two of the humans for a...colleague."

"Didn't you just lose an entire settlement? Why just these girls?"

He ignored her, his yellow eyes boring into her own. "Do you know anyone called Laney and Jane?"

Look down, look down, her mind chanted. *He'll see...*

A frown began to form on his forehead. "Are you wearing *one* contact lens?"

Hastily, she shoved a finger against his lips, desperately trying to ignore how it felt against her skin. "Shush."

"Are *you* Jane?"

Why had he assumed she would be Jane?

"I'm Laney."

"Huh, Quin didn't say you were a doctor. He also said Laney was the sensible one, Jane was the intellectual one. You don't seem to be doing the smart thing right now."

She ignored the taunt. *"Quin* sent you?"

The were tilted his head to one side, as if listening to something, then as fast as he'd stood, returned to his position on the floor. He gave her a lopsided grin before allowing his head to loll. A few seconds later, the outer door opened and the guard returned. He seemed amused at her position, huddled by the bars, and gave a slight chuckle.

Then the guard smiled. "Tatiana says to bleed him."

CHAPTER FOURTEEN

*I want super-speed, and maybe super-hearing. I
could skip the super-smell, though. People don't
tend to wash too frequently anymore.*
~ Quin Kirkman, Journal

Wolf could still smell the human woman even
though she'd been gone for hours. Cinnamon
and warmth, that's what she smelled like. He
felt as weak as a newborn pup, but he'd regain
his strength, even though the asshole guard
hadn't given him a liver to help him heal. But as
a second generation were, he could heal quicker
than they probably expected. At least, they
hadn't seemed to realize he was more powerful
than he'd let on. Although, he was still lying on
the concrete floor, in the same position they'd
left him. He'd used up his reserves of energy
when he'd all but jumped the woman – Laney.

"I wish they'd let me nibble on that pretty

human's neck," the vampire said into the stale air of their small prison. "She smelled amazing."

Something in Wolf almost snapped. He felt his body jerk in response, a growl emerging before he even knew what was happening.

"Tsk tsk, dog-boy. I wouldn't show the other vampires you like her, or she'll become someone's dinner or worse."

Wolf didn't bother to ask what 'or worse' was. He had an imagination, unfortunately. And he didn't like her. He didn't even know her.

"I don't like her," Wolf said, rather lamely.

"Sure you don't. That growl was just for effect."

"I can see why they want to torture you," Wolf muttered.

The vampire barked a wheezing laugh. "Oh, really?"

"Yes; your oh-so-charming personality. Although, what I don't understand is why you're still alive. I would have thought Tatiana was clever enough to kill a leader once she's deposed him."

"I don't know what you're talking about."

"Come on, Marcus, I am not an idiot."

"You're a were, some would say the two things are synonymous."

Wolf quirked an eyebrow, which the vampire couldn't see, and said nothing. He didn't have a lot more to say. He had to focus on how to break out. And then rescue Laney and her sister.

Quin had somehow forgotten to mention that Laney was breathtaking. It wasn't necessarily how she looked – she was pretty, with warm skin, those brown eyes and her shiny dark hair – it was something about *her*. She had a vitality, a *presence*. He wondered what color her eye was under that contact. Maybe she was a Blue, to make him feel this…infatuation.

He was an idiot.

And Quin was a dick for not describing his sisters properly.

"They're good girls, they'll go with you if you mention my name," Quin had said.

"What do they look like?" Wolf had asked.

"Both have tanned or olive skin, Laney has…Brown eyes, but Jane has Hazel. Dark hair for Laney, lighter for Jane."

"Detailed," Trace had mumbled disapprovingly. "Are they pretty, fat, thin, tall, short?"

"What human is fat nowadays? They're my sisters. I don't know if they're pretty or not."

Don't know if they're pretty or not. Wolf snorted. Quin was a blind fool.

"She wants me to marry her," Marcus said.

Wolf's mind went blank. Laney wanted to marry Marcus? He hadn't heard her say *anything* like that to the vampire. "Who?"

"Tatiana. Who else?"

Right.

Wolf was losing it. Maybe the blood loss and

the silver poisoning were affecting him more than he thought they had.

Wait… "*Marry* you?"

Why would Tatiana want to do something like that?

"Yes, *marry* me." Marcus sounded defensive.

"But marriage is for *life*."

"Yes."

"Does she intend for your life to be very short?"

"Hah. John, you're freaking hilarious. No, she wants it because I'm also first generation. *If* she could get me to fuck her – which would be seriously doubtful – then the children we had would be powerful. I think losing her last kid sent her insane. Well, more insane."

"And she wants *another* kid? In this environment?"

"Did you miss the part where I said she was insane?"

They fell into a surprisingly comfortable silence. Wolf didn't think he'd ever like a vampire, but he found he had a grudging respect for Marcus. The man had tolerated being tortured and having his people stolen from him, yet he still had a sense of humor.

"Would you stop the war, if you could?" Marcus asked.

Without blinking, Wolf replied, "Yes."

"Same, but I don't see how we can."

"Unless both races no longer have to rely on

human blood and flesh, I don't see how it *can* stop."

CHAPTER FIFTEEN

There are some people who just need to be shot in the face. Quick, easy, efficient. One less problem to worry about...
~ Quin Kirkman, Journal

Laney found herself thinking about the were far too much. John, she'd heard him say to SV1. She'd spent more time with the vampire patient, and yet it was the yellow-eyed man she couldn't get out of her head. She was crazy.

When the guard came to collect her the next day, she followed almost eagerly. Jane's eyes had tracked her movements, worried. Laney hadn't looked back, hadn't tried to reassure her. She didn't want the guard to think that they were closer than what she'd already given away. Love was a weakness when it came to vampires.

"I need you to check on our guests," the

vampire said.

Laney nodded, acting dutiful. She hoped her heart wasn't pounding too hard. Maybe the vampire would just think she was afraid. That would be better than him realizing she was excited.

The guard didn't leave her this time, keeping close to her as she tended both victims. The vampire's wounds had not healed much, and so she gave them a clean and re-bandaged them.

"I can't do much else with the supplies we have," she explained.

The vampire guard nodded and shuffled her along to John's cell. She tried to be brisk and businesslike, but her fingers burned where they made contact with his bare skin. Her breathing accelerated slightly and she focused on keeping it even. It was something that both the were and SV1 would notice.

The were's wounds *may* have been slightly less blue-black than before, but she couldn't tell. Removing the bandages, she began to clean the bullet holes on autopilot. Overnight, she'd been thinking of ways to try and remove the silver from his body, because she doubted the bleeding would have gotten all of it. It was possible that her Gray ability may work...although, she hadn't ever tried to do something like this before.

When she'd worked in the lab, she'd often used her telekinesis for very delicate tasks, often on the atomic scale. It had kept their research running long after much of the technology had been lost. While it hadn't been part of her direct study, she remembered what a silver atom was meant to look like, and she was very familiar with the structure of blood cells…and, well, she was probably kidding herself.

But she could try.

Without wanting to give herself away, she began to focus her ability on his body, trying to tune it into the feel of silver. Then, in her mind, she pictured the silver ions and began trying to force them out through the unhealed wounds. John grew taut, muscles clenching, and groaned.

"What are you doing?" he moaned.

"Cleaning your wounds," she said, pressing down with the gauze with perhaps a little more force than necessary.

SV1 laughed. "Come on, even Mar–the other prisoner was better than this."

Laney ignored John's moans and kept trying to control the direction of the tiny silver atoms. She didn't know if what she was doing was working, but since the were was reacting, she figured it must be doing *something*. Hopefully not killing him.

When he began panting, Laney eased up, pulling the cloth away and trying to be discreet in checking the gauze. It did look like there were some tiny patches of shining silver. Throwing it away quickly, Laney sloshed some more saline on the wound and then re-bandaged them. She felt John's gaze locked on her.

After she finished, SV1 herded her from the room and returned her to the dormitory. "How is your sister's wound?" he asked.

Laney blinked. "Almost healed," she replied.

The guard nodded and disappeared behind the steel door, locking her back in with the other villagers. Turning, Laney headed down the long aisles of beds and toward her bunk.

"Getting a bit chummy there, aren't you?"

Laney paused in her shuffle. Looking over, she saw Linette, one of the older village women. "Excuse me?"

"You go off with those leeches two days in a row; you come back with no bite marks. What are you doing to prevent being bitten? You fucking that guard?"

Laney gasped, mouth dropping open.

"How–"

After all she had done for the villagers. She'd seen to nearly every one of them in the last week, making sure their bites were healing, checking up on their general health. And this was the reaction?

"Jealous, are you?"

Turning, Laney looked over at her sister. Jane had come to stand beside her, arms folded across her chest. The bandage on her neck a kind of badge of honor.

"Well?" Jane demanded.

Jane's level of tact was almost zero at the best of times. When Laney was being picked on…

"She's getting special treatment!"

"*She* is providing medical aid to all of us. So what if she gets some special treatment? Could *you* prevent one of us from bleeding to death or getting an infection through specialized medical knowledge?"

The woman's wrinkled face contorted in anger, but she didn't say anything.

"If it wasn't for Laney, I'd probably be dying from an infection right about now," Jane said, matter of fact.

"And my cough would be worse." That was from Margo, who'd shown signs of a cold. Laney had requested heat packs and some remedies that the vampires had on hand.

"Leave Laney alone," a chorus of voices said.

Suddenly, Laney and Jane were surrounded by those in support. Linette's criticisms were drowned out. Overwhelmed, Laney stood there, unable to process what was happening. People were standing up for her. Humans. If they knew she was really half-Graced, she doubted they'd be so welcoming...but, she couldn't stop the grateful look from spreading over her face.

CHAPTER SIXTEEN

I want to be the one to save my sisters, since the wolf managed to lose them, but I can't risk being captured. There's too much on the line.
~ Quin Kirkman, Journal

It was time.

Today was the day that Trace and Quin were going to break Wolf out, no matter what. But first, Wolf had to survive his 'interview' with Tatiana. He'd only met her once, back when his father had introduced Wolf to some of his 'lab buddies.' He'd been a mere pup then, and thankfully took after his mother's looks. Tatiana had been all smiles and subdued crazy; she had a mate, children and there'd been plenty of humans left. Sure, there'd been an unofficial war between humanity and its creations, but on the surface, everything had seemed okay.

He doubted time had been kind to her.

Three sets of footsteps grew louder as his visitors got closer to the cells. "Has he talked much?" Tatiana asked.

"No." That was from the guard who brought Laney.

Lying on the concrete floor, he took deep breaths and tried to make himself look sicker than he was. His wounds were still healing, but his blood no longer felt as if it were on fire. Perhaps the 'bleeding out' – or more accurately, the guard drinking from him – had worked. He should be strong enough to get out of here, although he wanted Tatiana as far away from him as possible when the time came. He'd be no match for someone of her age and strength.

The door opened to the basement prison and the stronger scents of blood, adrenaline and death entered, along with the faint scent of cinnamon. Two vampires and a human. But he knew that scent by heart now: Laney. His heartbeat accelerated slightly, even though he willed it to remain calm and steady. He couldn't believe how he reacted to the little doctor, but he was grateful she was the human he'd come to break out. He wouldn't have been able to leave her behind otherwise.

And he was accusing Tatiana of being a nutjob.

Turning his head to the side, he took in the three visitors. Tatiana was statuesque, with long auburn hair and bright violet eyes. The guard looked the same as ever: professional. Laney appeared even thinner than she had two days ago, but her Brown eyes were large in her face.

"Check on the vampire," the guard said to Laney.

Nodding, she walked quietly over to the cell door, where the guard let her in. Tatiana strode over to stand in front of the bars of his cell.

"What's your name?" Her voice was smooth as silk. Pity it hid the viper underneath.

Wolf glared at her, and after waiting a suitable amount of time, gritted, "John Smith."

Fast as a whip, she dropped to a squat and shot her arm through the bars. She had him by the throat in seconds. Wolf stayed limp. "I don't appreciate people who lie to me."

Wolf bared his teeth. "I don't appreciate being captured."

She let go of his throat with a flick of her wrist, but her eyes bored into his.

Standing so fast he missed it, Tatiana turned to the guard and Laney. "Keep him locked up. Once I've dealt with the traitor, I'll decide what to do with the dog."

The guard nodded. Laney was muttering something about allergies. Tatiana seemed to grow bored, her expression blanking. She shook herself back to the present. "Leave the girl with the dog, she can check his wounds. Bring the traitor."

The guard ushered Laney out of the vampire's cell. "I don't think it's wise to leave the human unattended with the were."

"You said you've done it before."

"But that was a few days ago, when the silver was killing him."

"Well, if he hurts the human, I'll rip him apart. Solution."

"Having a human doctor is very useful."

"Then turn her into a vampire. Later though."

He thought Laney's eyes would bulge out of her head at that statement. But to her credit, she remained silent. Seconds later, she was locked in the cell with him. The guard slung a groaning Marcus over his shoulder and followed Tatiana out. Wolf waited until he couldn't hear their footsteps anymore before rolling to his side and springing to his feet. Laney jumped back.

"You seem better," Laney said.

"I feel better." He advanced on her in the tight space. She backed up to the cement wall, but stood straight, her head tilted back, staring at him defiantly. He couldn't help himself. Leaning down, he slanted his mouth across hers, kissing her gently. She froze, not responding, but not pushing him away.

Pulling back, he met her searching gaze. "Why?" she asked.

"Because I wanted to."

"I'm your food. I thought there were rules about that." Her eyes narrowed.

"I don't think of you as food."

"Well, you've probably nibbled on my liver before."

"I would never–" He felt his gorge rising. He couldn't even *think* of her as food. She was too special, too unique to be dinner.

She lifted her shirt, showing faint scars on the right side of her abdomen. "I've been harvested from."

He held out a shaking hand, as if to touch the scars, but he couldn't. He just couldn't. "We have to–"

"I know." She dropped the shirt.

Running a hand over his hair, he cursed. "If only there was a way that weres didn't have to feed from humans. Could get what we needed from any piece of meat…"

A hand shot out, grabbing his bicep. He froze. It was wrong how much he enjoyed that touch. "You mean that?"

He frowned. "Of course I do."

"Get me out of here, find me some test subjects, and I'll do it."

Wolf laughed, a short bark. "Now that's ambitious."

"I was working in a lab on this very problem with my sister before the last towns were turned to rubble. With her help, I can do this."

"But there aren't any labs left."

"I have ways around it."

He wanted to believe her, he really did, but he just couldn't pin his hopes on her finding a cure for him, or his people.

CHAPTER SEVENTEEN

I don't think I could have kids. This isn't a world for innocence.
~ Quin Kirkman, Journal

Jane wasn't meant to know where Laney went or who she went to see when she was taken away. But she had a fair idea. It was only logical, after all, that the vampires had some kind of medical issue they needed sorted, and they didn't want the humans – or even some of the other vampires – to know about it. She hoped it revolved around their need to drink human blood, but she doubted it. There was probably some injured vampire in need of a stake removal or some such. Disappointing, but then, most of the genetically modified were.

Walking to the door, Jane peered out the window and watched as the guard who normally took Laney down to the basement strode by, hauling a semi-conscious man over his shoulder. The man was emaciated, but seemed to focus on her studying him through the door's small glass window. Their eyes locked, and for a moment, she thought he smiled. Which was odd.

But there was no Laney.

Frowning, Jane turned back to the room and took in the humans there. Laney seemed to somehow get along with most of them, and they liked her. Jane they tended to ignore and focus on only when Laney wasn't there to provide medical advice. Throughout the years living at the settlement, the villagers had 'tested' her to see if she had any active Graced abilities. Small accidents to see if she'd use telekinesis to save herself, outpourings of emotion to see if she reacted, and scrunched faces which potentially indicated some very nasty thoughts. But she had no active powers, unless you counted an eidetic memory, and so she always passed their tests. It didn't matter that Jane was more qualified than her sister, she didn't have the requisite 'people skills' required for the actual practice of medicine, and so people overlooked her.

While the door to the sleeping area was reinforced steel, the rest of the warehouse had concrete walls. They muffled a lot of sounds, but not all of them. Suddenly, the worn screams of someone echoed throughout the warehouse, even in the dormitory. The other women went silent at the cries of agony. Once the yells stopped, Jane went back to the door and watched the same guard emerge, dragging the unconscious vampire along with him.

Jane had a fair idea that Laney would soon be attending to that vampire, if they wanted to keep him alive.

Once the guard had disappeared down the hall, she realized that a new series of shouts was audible. But these sounded like they were coming from outside. The unmistakable sound of shearing metal penetrated the walls. Frowning, Jane pressed her ear to the glass on the door and listened. Through the shouting and gunfire, Jane thought she heard growls. Pulling away, she strode to the middle of the room and put two fingers in her mouth, emitting a piercing whistle. All the women stopped their movements and turned to stare at her. Some were glassy-eyed, still high from their latest vampire bite.

"For those of you who wish to leave, I suggest you get in line. The weres are here."

CHAPTER EIGHTEEN

*They say revenge is a dish best served cold. Who the
fuck would want to eat a cold dish of revenge? Serve
it up hot and hard, that's what I think.*
~ Quin Kirkman, Journal

Laney stared at John's chest, rather than looking
him in the eye. He'd *kissed* her. And she'd let
him. There must be something wrong with her
mentally for her to allow a predator to do that.
The lamb and the lion, she thought. Probably
the worst part was that she wanted to leap on
him and keep going. But that was even more
monumentally stupid.

He leaned down and rested his forehead
against hers. His skin was so deliciously warm
in the cold of the cells. "It makes me sick to think
that your liver has been on someone's dinner
plate."

"It's not just me, it's everyone who lives at

the settlements."

"There's a reason why we don't get to know the people who live there."

Laney nodded. What else could she do?

He swooped in and pressed his lips again to hers, firmly, before sitting down on the floor of the cell, legs spread and a pained look on his face. Seconds later, SV1 came through the door carrying the limp vampire. Another stake jutted from the prisoner's chest.

Laney rushed to the bars, trying to assess the damage to her patient. "You'll be lucky if he survives that one."

"No great loss," the guard replied. Dumping the patient in the cell, SV1 left the door open before walking across and unlocking the one to the were's cell. "Glad to see she's still alive. Although, I wouldn't have minded seeing Tatiana rip you apart."

Opening the cell, the vampire froze when his radio came to life. "Beta team to base camp. Intruders have been spotted outside the compound's perimeter. The walls have just *collapsed*." Even through the crackly static, she could hear the horror in the speaker's voice.

The guard gave Laney and John an angry look before turning to slam the door closed. Faster than she could blink, John leaped on the guard, the door clanging and rebounding off the other bars as they fought. She hadn't even seen the were stand. A sharp cracking sound reverberated throughout the cell and SV1 toppled to the floor.

Numbly, Laney stared at the fallen guard. "What did you *do*?"

"Snapped his back. It won't kill him, but will leave him out of action until he heals. Let's go."

"We can't leave him here." Laney remained rooted to the spot.

"The guard? Sure we can. We'll just lock him inside the cell."

"No, him." She pointed at the vampire lying prone on the bed.

"We're definitely leaving *him*."

"No, they'll just keep torturing him."

Ducking around John, aware he could have stopped her at any time, she ran into the vampire's cell. Quickly assessing the situation, she ripped the stake from the vampire's side. She didn't have time to bandage his wounds, not if the compound was under attack. She was going to have to feed him. Reluctantly, she began rolling the sleeve of her sweater up.

A strong hand grasped her wrist. "What are you doing?"

Looking into John's bright yellow eyes, she sighed. "I need to feed him, or he won't make it."

"You are *not* food."

"Unfortunately, yes I am." Jerking her arm, she tried to pull it free.

"You really won't leave without this leech?"

Laney shook her head. Useless Hippocratic Oath.

Shoving her aside, John shoved his wrist in the vampire's face. "Drink from me, or we leave you here to rot. Your choice."

Fast as a snake, the vampire struck. John winced and bared his teeth. She saw the vampire bite down over and over and couldn't help but gasp. It must have hurt John so much...

"Enough."

The vampire let go then hauled himself upright. Seeing how emaciated he was, it would have taken immense strength of will to stop feeding once given the taste of blood. A were's blood was meant to be a poor substitute for human; the man was probably still starving. John swayed on his feet slightly, then righted himself.

Still clutching the bloody stake, she strode from the cell and out into the area where the fallen guard lay. "Shall we drag him into the cell?"

Before she could finish the sentence, the vampire prisoner ripped the stake from her hand and slammed it into the guard. She heard the sound of crunching bone and gagged.

"We could have left him alive!" she screamed.

But her former patient met her gaze, his expression eerily calm. "Trust me, this is better than what he deserves."

John sighed. "Let's just get out of here."

CHAPTER NINETEEN

Can I be Trace when I grow up? Man is a scary asshole.
~ Quin Kirkman, Journal

A very large were was standing in the dormitory doorway. Screams and yells broke out behind him, and she heard the snarls of wolves and cats too close for comfort. So instead, Jane focused on the were who had smashed the reinforced steel door in as if it was paper. She estimated that he was six feet eight inches in height (give or take) and would weigh close to four hundred pounds; very little of it fat. Golden eyes swept over the villagers, and she tried to stand tall. He was very intimidating. Even she knew who this man was.

"Only nine of them will come," Jane said. "I have not been able to ask the male villagers."

Those yellow eyes met hers. "I'm only here

for two of you."

Jane blinked. "But there are ten of us, plus my sister, who will go."

She swore that the man sighed. "As long as a Jane and Laney are among the number, fine."

Jane swallowed. "Laney was taken away by a guard."

The were turned and hit the wall. Concrete crumbled from the impact. "Mother*fucker*."

Why the weres were just after Laney and her... Maybe Quin had sent them? Trying to mollify the huge were, she said, "I'm Jane."

"Well, not a total loss. I still need to find a friend of mine. Go with Wes, who will get you out of here." Trace stepped to the side and a skinny man stared at her. Jane nodded.

"Let's go."

◆

Trace raced through the halls, his stride eating up more distance than those of smaller weres. He'd searched almost the entire compound by the time he found Jane, and now he was getting worried. He still hadn't located Wolf, or come across Tatiana, which could mean any number of bad things.

Racing into a room he stopped short. There she was.

Tatiana.

She wore all black and was barking orders into her radio.

Swinging around, she narrowed her eyes and hissed. "You."

Grinning, he leaned back against the doorjamb, acting nonchalant. "Hello my lovely, I've come back for my property."

"I am *not* your lovely."

Tatiana launched herself at him, and she was fast. Hands extended like claws, she almost succeeded in ripping out his throat. Ducking to the side, he grabbed her shoulder and swung around, using her own momentum against her. He slammed her into the concrete wall behind him. The sound of crunching bone and the smell of blood came to him. Hissing and spitting, she spun, her face smeared with crimson and her nose broken flat. Her nails scored long lines of pain across his chest before she drew her hand back to hit him. With her strength, she could probably punch a hole right through his chest.

Ducking low, he swept a leg out, knocking her off her feet. Then, leaping forward, he grabbed her head in both hands and turned. She resisted, but he was strong for a second generation were. A sharp sound echoed through the now still chamber and her body fell still.

The radio crackled to life and he didn't think he'd ever been happier to hear Wolf's voice. "Trace, you had better be here. I'm on my way out."

Reaching a hand down her side, he unclipped the radio from her belt. He spoke into the receiver. "Trace here. Just tidying up some loose ends."

Trace really should kill her. She was nothing but trouble, would keep coming after them, especially now that they'd stolen some of the humans back...

"Hurry the fuck up," Wolf barked.

Regretfully, Trace flicked a handful of Tatiana's thick auburn hair. Those oversize violet eyes stared up at him, fury and something else emanating from their depths. He chucked Tatiana under her pixie chin. "Until next time."

CHAPTER TWENTY

*I think the Raven Clan need a reminder they aren't
the most powerful group alive.*
~ Quin Kirkman, Journal

Wolf emerged with Laney and Marcus into the central courtyard. Laney hurried in front, while Wolf half-carried the vampire with him. A line of humans stood waiting in the area, surrounded by weres and the scattered remains of half a dozen or so vampires. At the head of the humans stood a tall and painfully thin woman who had a facial resemblance to Laney. She was talking to Wes, a were-panther.

"Who is *that*?"

Wolf looked down at Marcus and frowned. "Who is who?"

"The woman at the front." Marcus sniffed the air. "She smells even better than your doctor."

Laney spun around, and pointed a sharp

finger at Marcus' face. Her expression was almost murderous. "Touch her, and I'll make those stake wounds seem like a walk in the park. Got it?"

He hadn't thought he could be any more impressed by the human. He was wrong. A grin spread across his face.

Marcus smirked, then turned to Wolf. Their faces were far too close, since Wolf was keeping the vampire upright. "If you get a hard-on while holding me, I'll get worried about our relationship."

Wolf dropped the vampire.

"Ow."

Laney nodded and strode away, toward her sister. Jane smiled when she spotted the doctor.

"A little help?" Marcus held up a hand.

"I should leave you here to die."

"But your human doesn't want that."

Wolf helped Marcus up, then handed him over to a were guard, Todd. "Don't kill him."

Todd grimaced and held the vampire as if he was diseased. Wolf ignored the quips that were already emerging from the half-dead leech. Two vans came to a stop beside the line of humans, and Wes herded them into the vehicles. Wolf wanted Laney to ride with him, but she went with her sister without a backward glance. Grunting, he followed and climbed into the van's front seat. There was no partition into the back, so he could see her huddled with her sister, talking quietly, looking up every few seconds out the windows.

"Where are you, Trace?" Wolf muttered.

Over twenty black-clad vampires began to approach in the distance at a dead run, which didn't leave them much time. And Wolf didn't even have a gun to shoot the fuckers. Then Trace was there, bolting from one of the warehouse buildings and leaping into the open van door. "Let's get out of here."

Bullets began roaring through the air, but none seemed to touch the vans. Good thing the vampires were bad shots.

Trace slammed the door shut, eyes seeming to follow the paths of the misaimed bullets. "What's going on? Is Quin here? I told that fucker to stay back after he got us inside."

"Go, go, go!" Wolf shouted. Once the van engines were roaring, he turned back to Trace, who had blood running down his chest through a shredded shirt.

Looking into the back of the van, he saw Laney pressed close to the glass window, her eyes locked on the scene they were leaving behind. She was pale and shaking, her eyes focused. A chill began to spread over him.

Suddenly, Trace's question made sense. Wolf had a sinking feeling he'd just discovered the color of Laney's other eye.

"Laney, stop!" Jane began shaking her sister, but the doctor's eyes were focused on the scene outside the window. Blood was seeping out of Laney's nose.

Leaping over the seats, Wolf dove into the back of the van, squatting next to Laney and Jane. Jane turned to him, her Hazel eyes wild. "Stop her, she'll hurt herself. She can't do this much!"

"Have to get out of here," Laney muttered, a frown marring her brow. Blood began to pour from her nose, and he could see it start to drip from her ears.

Wolf grabbed her, but Laney ignored him, focusing on the bullets they were speeding farther and farther from. About to shake her, he watched as her eyes rolled back in her head and she collapsed.

"Laney!"

Cradling her to his chest, Wolf felt panic gnaw at him. Her body was limp in his arms, all her vitality *gone*. Raising a trembling hand, he felt for her pulse. It was there, thready, but there. Relief surged through him.

Then the sound of crumbling concrete and shearing metal reached his ears, and Wolf looked up to see warehouses fall to the earth in the background. The earth itself groaned, tremors making the van shake. Wolf felt the blood drain from his head. Quin had obviously decided to stop waiting.

How powerful *was* the man?

◆

Laney woke to a pounding head.

"Here." Someone slid a hand under her shoulders and propped her upright. A groan escaped her in protest.

"You need to drink."

She *was* thirsty. But her head hurt so much...

Gently, someone helped her take a few sips of room-temperature water. Nothing had ever tasted so good. Her helper lowered her back to the mattress and she shut her eyes, grateful. Hopefully they'd made it out of the compound. She'd used the limited skills she had to keep the bullets away, but it had put too much strain on her mind and it had given way. She was lucky she hadn't done herself more harm than a pounding head; at least, that's what she hoped.

Then, into the quiet that had soothed her poor mind, a familiar voice spoke. "You should have said you were a Gray."

It took her a few moments to process what John had said. "Why?"

"It's something essential about you."

Laney somehow managed a snort. "Because we shared those kind of details in our visits. Is your name even John?" It was an odd name for a were.

Warm fingers grabbed her chin, holding her head still. "I want to know everything about you. And my name is Wolfgang – Wolf."

Despite the pain in her head, warm tingles spread through her. "This isn't going to work."

"What isn't?"

"This." Laney waved a vague hand through

the air. She wanted to shake her head, but he held it still. Wolf brushed a feather-soft kiss against her mouth, electrifying her skin and making her forget about her pounding head.

"It seems to work well." His words were deep, rough.

"No, it will just end badly." Mostly for her. She was the human.

"Why can't it work?"

"I'm your food source."

"*You* aren't food. You don't have to go back to the settlement." He gave her a lopsided grin. "We could do with a doctor here."

"I'm not about to play *that kind* of doctor."

He let go of her chin and brushed strands of her hair from her forehead. So gentle. Ever since she'd first had contact with him, he'd treated her like porcelain. And now he was acting like she was the most precious thing in his world.

"You could become Bitten." The comment was offhand, but she knew he meant it. He was as taut as a bowstring.

"I might not survive."

"One of your eyes is Brown. You'd have a fifty percent chance of making it. Just as much as a Hazel, and they normally do."

But she was different. She had heterochromia, and if she was Bitten, she could end up in who knew what state. Maybe she'd only half turn, making her into a nightmare to scare children. "I don't want to feed off humans. I don't think I could live with needing to eat human liver."

His expression dulled. "You won't even try to see if it could work?"

"How can it?"

Leaning down, he pressed his forehead to hers, tender. "Because it has to."

CHAPTER TWENTY-ONE

I have a plan. My sisters may hate me for it, but it's the only humane way forward. We – the Graced – could end this war right now, but so many people would die. I want to save as many as I can. If I can. I just have to get the others to agree. I know Gemma Frost is on board.
~ Quin Kirkman, Journal

It had been almost six months since they'd broken Laney, Jane and the nine other women out from the vampire compound. Quin had vanished once he'd been convinced his sisters were safe. Off to wherever Graceds disappeared to.

So much for their deal.

"Did you hear about what happened today?" Wolf asked Marcus.

The three of them, Marcus, Trace and Wolf, were sitting in Wolf's small office. It had never felt more spacious than it had since he returned from his concrete and steel cell. Although, the three of them certainly made the area feel cramped. Wolf kicked his feet up on his desk. His office, his rules. The other two looked at his raised legs with resentment. They did look a little restricted. Wolf grinned.

When he'd brought the vampire back to the compound, he'd half expected to kill the leech when Laney wasn't looking and leave it at that. But Marcus had been injured and largely feeble, and well, Wolf had felt sorry for him – aside from Laney's mutterings about patient care and what not. Who even knew the Hippocratic Oath was still taken seriously with humans becoming a rare species? Either way, pity was a weakness in a clan leader, but he'd allowed it. And now he had a new buddy.

It was almost galling.

Marcus gave a depreciating smile. "That I failed yet again in my attempts to woo the lovely Jane?"

"That's old news." Wolf waved a dismissive hand. "This is even better."

Trace folded his arms across his broad chest.

"Trace is being *courted*."

"Fuck off." Trace's frown turned thunderous.

Wolf laughed. It felt good. He hadn't done enough of it lately. "A liver was left in a box out near the compound this morning. Trace's name was carved into the lid." He grinned. "It was a bit off before we got to it, though. And it was a vampire's."

Marcus eyed Trace. "What did you do to make Tatiana *like* you? I assume it's Tatiana. Didn't you say you snapped her neck?"

"Maybe she gets off on the whole 'let's kill each other' thing," Wolf suggested.

"I am going to have to fake my death. This is the sixth present she's sent me since we got the humans out, and she hasn't retaliated. Normally we'd be at full-blown war."

"Maybe you should just put out to keep them out?" Marcus said.

Trace growled. "That from the man who was staked over and over again because he wouldn't fuck the crazy leech."

"No way was I producing offspring with that psychopath. And that's saying a fair bit coming from me." Marcus nodded to himself. "But it's not like you have the risk of getting her pregnant."

Marcus hadn't exactly had the cleanest of reputations. But then, you couldn't be a clan leader and remain pristine. Wasn't in the job description. But Tatiana did make him look like a do-gooder.

Trace shook his head. "I don't want anything precious of mine near her. She might rip my cock off in some convoluted revenge for me breaking her neck."

Someone tapped at the door. "Knock knock."

The three of them turned to look at the

intruder and Wolf's jaw dropped. "Odo?"

Right there in the corridor was his brother, Odolf. The lanky were was leaning against the doorjamb as if he hadn't a care in the world. Wolf hadn't seen his brother in years – Odo was a lone ranger if ever there was one. Wolf sprung to his feet and leaped over the desk, coming to stand before his sibling. He slapped the other man on the back.

"Odo!" Trace also stood.

Odo gave a careless grin and waved at the bear, but did a double take when he spotted Marcus. A low growl emerged from his brother's chest.

"Why is there a leech in your office? Without chains?" Odo's voice was rough, hackles up.

Wolf shook his head. "Long story, but he's safe. Anyway, what are you doing here? Staying for long?"

The two of them had a generally uneasy relationship. Mostly because Wolf wanted Odo to stay with the clan and be safe, whereas Odo wanted to wander free and be unconstrained. Plus, Odo wasn't as dominant as Wolf, so was lower in the pecking order. That had never sat well with the other werewolf. But Wolf still missed him.

Looking at Odo was like looking in a mirror, although one with a different color palette. They were almost identical, except Odo had white-blond hair to Wolf's blond-brown and white skin to Wolf's tan. They both had the same golden-yellow eyes, though. And Odo's were still locked suspiciously on Marcus.

"No, I won't be staying long. But I thought I'd drop off my son."

Wolf felt his jaw drop. Saw Trace's do the same. "Son?"

Odo turned and shouted down the corridor, "Boy!"

Blinking, Wolf saw a lanky youth skulk toward them. Hands in his pockets, hair wild about his face, it was uncanny how much the lad looked both like Odo and himself. Although far more sullen.

Odo stood next to the lad, awkward. "This is my son."

"You said the word 'son,' but I'm still not getting it." Wolf ran a hand over his face.

"What are you talking about? The boy looks just like you two," Marcus said, ever helpful. "Maybe he's your son, Wolf."

The youth's eyes went wide at the sight of the vampire, and he cowered a little behind Odo. Although, Wolf could tell there was no real love between the father and son duo.

"Apparently I knocked his mother up about twenty years ago. Went through the area a month or two back and spotted the kid. Most of the clan was dead. He'd been living pretty rough."

Twenty years old. The poor boy only looked about fifteen he was so skinny. Living in a ghost town...no wonder the lad was wary. And typical Odo would have just grabbed the kid without too much in the way of explanation and hightailed it.

"I can't look after a kid," Odo continued. "So I thought I'd drop him here, let the clan raise him. How it should be."

No, that wasn't how it should be. That only happened if you were an orphan. Something like anger flashed in the youth's eyes, but his mouth remained compressed in a thin line.

Odo looked at the three of them, standing crammed in the entrance of Wolf's office. "I'll let you settle him in, I'm going to get a shower. Catch you later, boy."

With that, Odo turned and wandered off down the hall, whistling. When he was out of earshot, Marcus scratched his head. "Is it just me, or was that whole conversation completely fucked up?"

Wolf's reply was automatic. "Language."

"Because the kid's never heard the word 'fuck' before." Trace shook his head.

The boy remained silent.

Wolf turned to him, tried his best 'nice guy' smile. Kid didn't seem to buy it, from the stony expression on his face. Smart.

"What's your name?" Wolf asked into the quiet.

"Clay. Clay Lovett."

Not his or his brother's surname, interesting.

"Well, Clay. I'm Wolfgang – Wolf for short." Wolf extended his hand out for a shake. "That big hulking idiot is Trace, and the fanged moron is Marcus."

Clay took Wolf's hand, a little tentative at first, but with strength. "Nice to meet you. I think."

♦

"That vampire won't leave me alone." Jane scrunched her face as she turned to look at Laney.

Laney bit the inside of her cheek to prevent herself from smiling. The two of them were standing in the half-working lab that belonged to the base Wolf had appropriated. It had been wonderfully intact, even with a computer that ran off the generated power. Jane had actually laughed with glee when she'd spotted it. The rest Laney had been able to manipulate with her telekinesis to get it working.

"The *vampire* is a first-generation ex-clan chief." Who had recovered from his multiple stakings surprisingly well. He had scars, but then, so did Wolf. The were had small, puckered blue-black marks, showing the bullet wounds and the tissue that had never recovered properly.

"He's annoying."

He's smitten, Laney wanted to say, but she kept quiet.

It was rather amusing to watch *the* Marcus Kipling trip all over himself trying to impress

Jane, only to fail on every level he could. The only time he could get her interested in him was when he was volunteering his blood and body for their experiments. All the suave and charm he normally exuded were useless on her sister. Suffice to say, he seemed to be *very* interested in their progress.

"Are you ready to tell them?" Jane asked.

"Guess I have to be." Their 'vaccine,' as they called it, was ready. Thanks to all the mental exercises and gedanken experiments they'd run back in the settlement, they'd managed to cut years off their research. Although, they'd already been working on this particular problem for a good eight years before that. And had based their research off a hundred years of earlier experimentation.

"Tell us what?" Wolf strode into the lab like he owned it. Then again, he did.

"We're ready to begin trials," Jane announced.

Laney hadn't had to say anything in the end anyway.

Marcus and Trace were right on Wolf's heels, as was a malnourished-looking youth. Features that were scarily familiar looked at her from that thin face. Wolf stopped, shoved his hands in his pockets, and looked a little uncomfortable. "This is my long-lost nephew, Clay."

Marcus ignored the introduction and was eyeing Jane like a tasty treat. Jane took a couple of steps closer to Laney. "He's staring at me again," she whispered.

"He can hear you," Laney replied.

Marcus flushed a pale pink – which was quite the blush for a vampire – and stared at his boots. Trace laughed.

"Hey, I wouldn't laugh if I was you," Laney said. "I hear you're quite popular nowadays."

"Would you all just shut up about that?" Trace grumbled without heat. While Laney still found the monstrous man slightly terrifying, he'd only ever been kind to her and Jane. He raised his eyes to the ceiling.

"So who're the guinea pigs?" Wolf asked. "Aside from my charming self."

That had been one of the stipulations when they first began. Wolf or Trace would have to be one of the subjects, being second generation. But only one of them. If something went wrong, they couldn't afford to lose both alphas.

"We have a list. You can go first, though," Laney said. She was nervous. If this worked, then the barriers she'd managed to erect between them would fail. They joked about Tatiana and Marcus courting Trace and Jane, but Wolf had been the most relentless. While Laney refused to take their relationship further due to their species, he would constantly seek her out, kiss her when her guard was down, and go to extremes to get her to simply laugh. Sometimes, they just sat and talked. He was funny, smart, and loyal as anything. She didn't know why he wanted her.

Crazily, she loved him. And she wanted to be with him so badly she'd cry herself to sleep at night. But she couldn't begin something that would just end when she began to age and he grew bored. Or, he might use her affection for him to Bite her and make her a were. She couldn't do that, not when humans were still their only food source.

Jane loaded a syringe full of the gene-altering virus and handed it to Laney. Wolf pulled up a chair and rolled up his sleeve, exposing a bicep. The fingers of her free hand curled, wanting nothing more than to stroke all that glorious skin and muscle.

She quickly swabbed the area with alcohol, then injected the syringe. Once it was done, she released her breath, and realized everyone else had been holding theirs too.

"What did you just do?" the boy asked into the quiet, as they all studied Wolf to see if anything was going to happen.

"We injected him with a gene–" Jane began.

Laney interrupted. "We made a drug that will hopefully mean he no longer has to rely on human liver. That his body will be able to process the nutrients from animal flesh. Any animal flesh."

Jane blinked. "If you don't want to be technical about it, yes."

"Lack of technical mumbo jumbo is good," Trace said.

"You can talk technical all you want to me."

Marcus gave a megawatt grin.

Jane glowered at him and held up another needle. "Here."

Marcus sidled over to her with a hopeful look. She frowned even harder at him. "You get one too." Jane jabbed the vampire in the arm with less finesse than Laney had Wolf. And no alcohol swab. She was cranky.

"Ow."

"He's not a were," Trace said.

"No, but he was annoying and kept giving me blood samples." Jane put the syringe down and turned to her computer. She began typing notes rapidly. "So I made one for vampires, too."

Silence.

"Did you hear that? She just whipped up the salvation for my people?" Marcus turned to Jane, who was still typing notes. "Will you marry me?" he blurted.

"No."

"Let me take you on a date?"

Jane didn't even look up. "A date? Where to? The cells? No."

"Kiss my arm better?"

Jane sighed. "It's already healed."

Laney laughed.

A gentle hand touched her arm and she jolted. Wolf spoke quietly, "How long until we know it works?"

"How long until you normally starve from not eating human liver?"

"We start to feel the effects after a week or two."

"Give it a month with a game diet. See how we go."

"You are amazing, you know that?" Wolf's eyes were serious. His whole body leaned toward her.

She shrugged, tried to act natural. "Just doing my job."

He crushed her in a hug. It was so unexpected she squeaked. She felt everyone's eyes turn to them, then heard Trace herding the others out of the lab. Jane protested, but Marcus made some sleazy comment that left her spluttering.

Wolf loosened the hug and framed her face in his hands. "I can't keep pretending that I don't admire you, that I don't love you. I know you don't want to try, but I do. Even if this drug doesn't work, even if you have to stay human, I still want to *try*."

Laney's heart broke. Raising a shaking hand, she touched his mouth. "I–"

"No, don't say anything because you feel you have to. But know that I will wait for you forever if I have to. I love you, Laney. You're in my soul, if I have one."

She burst into tears.

Wolf made shushing sounds and gathered her in his arms. She cried for a long time, but her fear bled out as she did so. Hiccupping, she wiped the tears from her cheeks and raised puffy eyes to meet his steady and concerned gaze.

"I love you, too. But I don't think I can ever eat human liver. It's why I've been working so hard on the vaccine."

He brushed tears she'd missed from her cheeks. "I know. We'll make it work."

EPILOGUE

A year later…

"If you keep moving, I won't be able to cut it straight. Or I might lop off your ear." Laney tried to keep her voice stern as she spoke to Clay, but the were kept wriggling around. He was so adorable with his puppy-dog eyes and his floppy hair that she didn't really want to give him a haircut, but it had to be done.

He was too cute for his own good.

As Odo had taken off and left his son behind, Laney had worried about the boy's mental stability. But he'd taken to clan life like a duck to water, and Wolf had been a huge part of his nephew's attitude. And it was stupid of her, thinking of him as a boy. Clay was only six years younger than herself, but weres aged differently, and while Clay had seen horrors, he still had an innocence to him that Laney had long lost. She hoped he managed to keep it forever.

"Just do it with your telekinesis, no scissors needed then."

Laney snorted.

Just as Laney was about to cut a rather large chunk of hair, Jane strode into the lab with a loud, "Okay!"

Putting the scissors down, Laney eyed her sister. She seemed strangely cheerful. "I have now inoculated every were we could track down. There will be more, but if they breed with those who have had the vaccine, then the vaccine-altered genes should pass down to the offspring."

Jane hadn't *personally* injected every were on the continent, but they had spread the vaccine as far and wide as possible. Quin, who had returned after his six-month absence, had also helped. He'd also started stalking vampires, and using his Gray abilities to inject them from afar with darts. So far, they'd probably managed to vaccinate over half the remaining vampire population. It was only so easy because there were only thousands left of each. If it had been pre-Civil War, then their vaccine would never have stood a chance.

Clay turned to Laney. "So what will you do now?"

"What do you mean?" Laney put the scissors away in a drawer, his hair still long and shaggy.

"Now your life's purpose has been obtained?"

Laney's hands came to a stop. It had been a year since Wolf had had to eat human flesh. Eight months since everyone else in the clan had had to, either. Three months since she'd agreed to be Bitten. Her fears hadn't been remiss – she hadn't come out of the change a complete were. Her Gray eye was still Gray, her Brown eye now yellow. And she couldn't shift; her animal was trapped within. It clawed at her, but she was getting used to the pain. Maybe her next goal could be working out how to enable her wolf to be free.

"That is something she needs to work out, you nosy brat." Jane patted Clay affectionately on the head.

It was strange, seeing her sister with Clay. Jane still largely ignored most of the weres, except for the lad. They'd bonded, over what, Laney couldn't guess. But Clay seemed to have an irresistible charm that she knew was going to cause problems. She'd even seen Marcus quizzing the youth on what he'd done to get Jane to smile at him.

Although, as Jane's work *was* largely completed, Laney had seen her looking around for a new task. Jane had to be busy. Laney had the sneaking suspicion Marcus may just become her sister's new project. Not that he'd be much of a challenge, not when he was already head over heels. Laney might have to tell him to play hard to get for a while. It'd confuse Jane, and that was never a bad thing.

Wolf entered the lab then, Quin close on his heels. Laney gave them both a bright smile.

"Did Jane give you the news? We're done!" Wolf picked Laney up and spun her round, planting a searing and too quick kiss on her lips.

"Almost," Laney and Quin said.

"Almost?" Wolf frowned.

Laney looked at Quin, who met her gaze with his steady Gray eyes. They'd talked about it, argued about it for months. But there wasn't any other solution they could see, and even Jane agreed. And if there was anything Jane was protective about, it was memory and knowledge. Plus, the others had already decided.

Laney looked at the floor. "We managed to save your race, the vampires, and the humans, but there's still the Graced."

"They aren't food anymore, either," Clay protested.

"No, but they're still hunted," Quin said. "We're going extinct."

Wolf shook his head. "We have a deal. We leave your people alone."

"You may, but not everyone has the same deal. We can't afford to be hunted anymore, not for our abilities, not for our breeding capacity. We're going to start saving ourselves." Quin took a deep breath. "It's a two-pronged attack. We're going to erase the memories that Graceds even exist. There are a few Greens left who are strong enough to do it. We've talked about it, and agreed. Any were, human or vampire will have all knowledge of the Graced wiped from their mind. They'll just become regular humans to them. Any who escape the wipe will receive due warning: choose to forget us, or die."

"No!" Clay stood. "I don't want to forget *anything* about Laney or Jane!"

Quin looked over at Clay, and her brother's gaze was ancient. Quin was only six years older than Laney, but he seemed centuries wearier in that instant.

Wolf put a hand on Clay's shoulder. "Can the boy be spared?"

"I'll vouch for him, Quin," Laney said softly.

"Your memory-thing won't happen overnight," Wolf warned. "This won't result in instant protection."

"You'd be surprised how quickly it can be done. The Greens can do it remotely, since it's only one memory they're taking. I'm not going to watch my people die out while everyone else gets the chance to finally thrive." Quin's voice was hard.

Wolf looked at her. "You agreed to this madness?"

"I'm half-Graced." She touched the skin just below the lower eyelid of her right eye. "If it wasn't for my ability, we'd have never been able to make the vaccine, because the technology is almost gone. In another ten years, we'll probably have lost the last computer. I'm not going to let my people go extinct."

Wolf hung his head. "We don't have a choice, do we?"

"Some of your people will escape the memory wipe because of natural shields. I know you and Trace have them. This was more of a courtesy call than a request for permission." Turning slowly, Quin headed from the room. "I understand if you want our alliance to end."

"No," Wolf said, hand still on his nephew's shoulder. "We still stand together. For those who will remember." He paused. "What was the other 'prong' of your attack?"

"We're going to destroy the compounds and fortresses. All of them."

Wolf sputtered, a growl rising from deep within his chest.

"New beginnings for everyone," Laney said softly. "Everyone starts again, so that technology is no longer a weapon that can be used against *anyone*."

Wolf exploded across the room, pacing furiously. "But this is our home!"

"Because of our deal, you get a reprieve," Quin said. "I will spare you and your clan as long as I can, but eventually, all of this will fall." He waved a hand around the room.

Laney didn't doubt her brother. She'd heard about the devastation he'd wrought once Laney and Jane had made it out of the Raven Clan's compound. She'd never realized how strong he was.

Quin turned back and came to stand in front

of Laney. Pride was in his gaze, as was sorrow. "I want you to know that there are some Graceds who are planning on hunting all half-breeds down. Not Hazels, but those who are half-Graced, half-vampire or were. Stay hidden as long as you can. I will protect you for as long as I live, but now that isn't going to be long enough. I love you, no matter what species you are. Keep safe."

Tears streamed down Laney's cheeks and her heart swelled.

As Quin turned to leave the room, he met Laney's and Jane's gaze. "I love you both, even though I'm more absent than present."

"We love you too," Laney said, voice clogged with tears. Jane nodded, seeming lost for words. Tears tracked unnoticed down her sister's cheeks. Why did this feel like a good-bye?

When Quin reached the doorjamb, Laney met Clay's troubled gaze. "What about Clay's memory?" He was only a child, in the scheme of things.

Quin's expression was sad as he looked at them, standing clustered together in the lab that had changed the fate of the world. "The boy must have a strong natural shield, otherwise he'd have already forgotten."

Turning away, Quin walked out of the room. Quietly, so quietly he probably didn't think they'd heard, he said, "But that may be more of a curse than a blessing."

♦

Humanity created three of the four races that now call this world home; yet they couldn't control what they made.

But we can.

And we will not tolerate disobedience. Let the vampires and weres build their compounds, to once again enslave the remaining humans.

I'll just destroy anyone who dares to try.

~ Quin Kirkman, Journal

ACKNOWLEDGMENTS

Captive was inspired by my friends and readers. So many people reached out and asked about Clay's history, so I wanted to give readers a snapshot of what the world was like when he was a youth. So firstly, I want to thank those of you who read *Graced*, and liked it enough to contact me! Also, I'd like to thank my husband Tom, and my wonderful beta readers: Liz Grzyb and Joanne Danton. All your thoughts and comments made this book better.

I also want to send out a huge thanks to my amazing agent, Jenny Darling, and the team at Momentum: Haylee Nash, Michelle Cameron, Julia Knapman, and Ashley Thomson: you were an absolute delight to work with.

Amanda Pillar is an award-winning editor and author who lives in Victoria, Australia, with her husband and two cats.

Amanda is the author of the Graced series, and has had numerous short stories published. She has co-edited six fiction anthologies and solo-edited two: *Bloodstones* and *Bloodlines*, published by Ticonderoga Publications.

In her day job, she works as an archaeologist.